Produced by LouLou Productions LLC
Copyright © 2012 by David Carner
Cover design by R. Carner

Paperback ISBN: 978-0-9859514-6-7

To find out more about John Fowler, please feel free to follow my author page on Facebook. The David Carner fan page currently holds all announcements pertaining to this series. Also check out www.davidcarner.com for information on this series and any other works. You may also follow me on twitter @davidcarner.

The John Fowler Novels

The Road to Justice

Sins of the Son

This Thing of Ours

Journey's End (Coming Christmas 2013)

Day's Past (Coming Christmas 2014)

Check out http://david-carner.blogspot.com/ for my free short story, Bad Day in Queen's Landing. The blog is updated with a new chapter weekly.

Four Days Ago

Chapter 1

The FBI agent sat in a stolen car watching prostitutes work the street corner. He had been waiting patiently for a certain call girl to show up. Her name used to be Tiffany. He had no idea what her name was now, and he really didn't care. As the agent sat on stakeout, he ran through his plan for the fifth time that night. He had been trained by his father to always plan when you could, and he wanted his dad's approval more than anything in the world. He saw Tiffany walk up to the corner. The agent smiled, started the car, and pulled up to the curb. He pointed toward Tiffany, and she walked up to the car. The agent pulled out a roll of ten $20 bills. Tiffany smiled, opened the door, and got in the car. The agent pulled away from the curb with a destination in mind.

"You gotta name, Sugar?" Tiffany asked.

"You don't remember me?" the agent asked. "It's John, John Fowler. I used to see you all the time when you worked at that strip club, The Daily Grind Gentleman's Club."

Tiffany looked the agent up and down and shook her head.

"Sorry, Sugar, I don't remember you. I remember the name, but you don't look like I thought you should. Sorry," she said regretfully.

"That's ok," the agent said, his bright blue eyes sparkling. "I hope this isn't weird. I always thought you were hot back when we worked at the club, but I never mixed business with pleasure."

Tiffany smiled. "Not a problem, Sugar. Where are we going?"

The agent smiled. "How about the old club? I can get us in."

"Ooh, kinky! I like it!" Tiffany giggled and sat back in the seat of the car. After a few minutes, they arrived at the abandoned strip club. The agent helped her through an opening in the back, and they made their way through the old club. It was still in good shape. The pole was the focal point of the room with all of the tables turned to face it. Most of the tables had seats on them. A layer of dust covered almost everything. There hadn't been any signs of vandalism, which didn't surprise the agent. You'd have to be pretty stupid to vandalize an old Mafia hangout. It had been abandoned for several reasons. The main one being that John Fowler helped put its former owner in jail four years ago. Tiffany took the agent's hand and giggled.

"The Champagne Room?" she asked. The agent smiled wickedly.

They headed into the room. It was pitch black. The agent reached into his coat and pulled out a flashlight. He turned it on, and the room lit up. Cheap vinyl chairs and couches that could easily be cleaned off littered the room. He sat the flashlight on the couch. He looked at the surface, wondering how many germs were on the couch, but he knew what he had to do. The agent sat down, and Tiffany crawled onto his lap. The agent smiled and made a turnaround sign with his index finger. Tiffany winked at him and playfully slapped his leg. Tiffany turned around and started to straddle him. The agent popped up off the couch in an instant, grabbed her head, and twisted it quickly. The agent smiled at the cracking sound her neck made. Her body dropped to the floor, dead. The agent looked down at the lifeless prostitute on the floor.

"Oops," Bruce said to her dead body. "I'm sorry I had to do that, but I needed to send John a message." Bruce leaned down to whisper into her ear. "Ok, you got me," he whispered. "I'm not really sorry, but don't tell anyone." Bruce began to ready the abandoned building to be burnt down, whistling and giggling as he did.

Over 5 Years Ago
Chet's Apartment, New York City

Chapter 2

Chet looked at his poker account for the third time in the past two minutes. $0.00 was showing in the balance. Just three minutes ago, it read $500,000.00. Chet had just moved all in on another player. He had trip aces, and his opponent had been semi-bluffing with a flush and straight draw. Chet had a 70% chance to win the hand going into the river. Chet knew the other player was bluffing. The guy he had been playing with believed in using his big stack to push other players around.

Chet couldn't believe his good luck. He was going to withdraw over $100,000.00 out of his poker account that night before he started checking the games that were going on. Chet knew he could beat his opposing player. All of that changed when his opponent's flush card came on the river, and Chet was left penniless.

Chet hadn't played the percentages, cards, or even the player wrong. He had just misplayed his bankroll. It was just too good of an opportunity, in his mind, for him to make a whole lot of money. Chet was crestfallen. Not only had he blown his entire bankroll, but he was going to use some of that money to cover rent that month. He had taken a bad beat at a local game earlier that week that had wiped out all of his cash. Chet was literally broke.

Chet walked around his apartment for a minute and thought about his options. He could call John and get a loan. John would help him and wouldn't say anything. The problem was all Chet could ask from John was enough to pay his bills. The best Chet could hope for online was to rebuild his bankroll from the one cent/two cent games. That would take forever. The other option was to call a loan shark he knew. Chet knew, since he was an FBI agent, he really shouldn't have contact with The Duck, but he could borrow enough to both get in on a decent game and pay rent.

Chet sat for a minute. He picked up the phone and dialed John's number but never hit the send button. Chet closed his eyes, hit erase, and punched in The Duck's number. Chet was only going to ask for $25,000.00. That would be plenty to get him started. The phone rang. When it was picked up, the only thing Chet heard on the other end was, "Quack." That was it, just one simple word to let people know who they reached.

"Duck," Chet began. "It's Chet Morris. How much am I good for?"

There was silence on the phone for a minute. Chet waited patiently. He heard some keystrokes.

"One cent," the voice on the other end finally said to Chet. Chet knew that meant one hundred thousand dollars. Cent stood for centomila, which in Italian meant one hundred thousand. Chet knew he shouldn't take more than twenty-five thousand, and even that was risky. He was somewhat surprised to hear his own voice.

"Can you transfer the whole amount into my account?" Chet asked.

"Quack," was the response, and the line went dead. Chet was positive that in three months, he would have the loan paid off. If not, he would tell John and they would straighten everything out. Chet checked his online bank account and saw the funds were already there. He loaded fifty thousand into his poker account and went back to playing. It would be no time before he paid off the Duck and took down his poker nemesis. No time at all.

Today
The Moores

Chapter 3

John stood at the top of the stairs at the Moore home. He looked into the family room where everyone he considered family, except for his parents, sat talking. He looked at Arthur and Madeline Moore, Sam's mom and dad. The Moores earned their initial money the old fashioned way; Arthur inherited it. John smiled and took a drink of tea. If you ever mentioned to Arthur how he came into his money, he would remind you how he had doubled the money ten times over. Arthur had taken his parents' money and managed to make them rich beyond John's dreams. John should know. Once Sam, his wife who died four years ago, passed away, John came into the entire inheritance of Arthur's parents. John thought he should really one day look into how much money was left to him.

Sitting close to the Moores was Rosa Martinez. She had been the former housekeeper of Archibald Staples. Archibald was the closest thing to a nemesis that John had, except for the person who killed Sam. Archibald was suspected of everything under the sun, but nothing had ever been, or could be, proven when it came to illegal activities concerning him. Until now. Archibald thought Rosa couldn't speak English when he hired her and spoke in front of her about everything. Rosa was hiding out at the Moores' until the FBI could finish interviewing her and build a case against Archibald. In the meantime, Rosa and Madeline were becoming joined at the hip.

John next looked at the soon to be former Senator, Jeremiah Cosby. John wondered if the country was ready for Jeremiah to become the Vice President of the United States. Jeremiah stood for truth and wanted to stamp out those who committed heinous acts. Most politicians thought Jeremiah was too strict, especially since Jeremiah was looking at cleaning up the way Washington worked. John remembered when he first met Jeremiah. John had thought Jeremiah to be out of touch with people. John had been at an event he was throwing when there was a commotion outside. The kitchen staff had caught what they called "a bum" going through the trash, looking for food.

Jeremiah had talked to the man, and to John's surprise, sent the man home with food for his family. The next week, Jeremiah had gotten the man a job. When John asked Jeremiah about it later, Jeremiah responded, "That man didn't fail society, my boy. We failed him. Well tarnation, young feller, why should I have all of this food and money I'll never use? It wasn't like the man was looking for a handout. He had offered to work for someone in the kitchen staff earlier this week, but they flat out refused to even let him clean up!" John had never told anyone that story; he wanted no part of politics. Jeremiah was a good man that wanted to serve the people, not a chosen few. John thought of Jeremiah as a second father. So did his late wife, Sam.

Sam. She was the reason they were all gathered here. It was getting close to four years now since her death, and her case still hadn't been solved. John still remembered walking home the night he had closed the big Mafia case and being so close to their apartment when it exploded, with Sam inside. John sucked on an ice cube and looked down at Chet, Trip, and Jessica. Somehow, it had gone from just him to him, Chet and Jessica. Well, somehow wasn't true. The creation of the team had been all Sam and Jeremiah's doing, but that was a story for another day. After Sam's death, John left the FBI. Recently, he came back, and now, instead of a team of three, it seems they had added in the New York Office

Director, Trip. John shook his head and chuckled to himself.

Chapter 4

John still wasn't sure when Trip had become more like a friend than a boss, but there wasn't any point denying it. Trip was known in the office as straight laced and by the book, but since Sam's death, something changed in Trip. John was told he was going to learn what changed this weekend. Whatever it was, it must have been a doozy. Right before they had all left to come to the Moores' to go over Sam's case file, a psychologist assigned to evaluate John had been murdered. Trip had gone to great lengths to keep it quiet. Trip believed the death was related to Sam's and to Thelma's deaths. Thelma had been Trip's kinda-sorta-not-really girlfriend. She had died just hours after getting information for Trip. The sad thing was that Trip never received whatever information Thelma had apparently died over.

John shook his head regretfully and looked over at his true best friend, Chet. Chet was so incredibly smart and had computer skills that John couldn't even comprehend. John had thought many times Chet could be the world's greatest hacker, programmer, or both. John smiled and chewed on another ice cube. He could barely turn on a computer or use his smart phone, while Chet could probably program his smart phone to drive a car. John didn't really know if that was true or not, but it wouldn't surprise him. A voice interrupted his thoughts.

"Why don't you take a picture?" Jessica asked. "It will last longer and be a bit less creepy."

Jessica had come up the steps without John noticing her. John turned toward Jessica, smiled, slipped his arm around her back, pulled her close, and kissed her. She immediately jumped back with a look of shock on her face. John laughed. He had forgotten about the ice cube he had been chewing on.

"Your lips are freezing," Jessica said. She took the cup away from John, tipped it up, and took one of the ice cubes in her mouth.

"What's wrong?" John asked. "A little too hot for you down there?"

"You'd like that, wouldn't you?" she replied. "Your . . . . what do you call them, ex-in-laws, widower-in-laws?"

"The Moores?" John offered. Jessica smiled and punched John lightly on the arm. John mouthed, "Ow," and rubbed his arm.

"You big baby," Jessica said, smiling at him. John had no idea how to classify his relationship with Jessica. He knew they were dating and that they were boyfriend and girlfriend, but after that . . . . well it was all so complicated . . . or maybe it wasn't.

John had been married to Sam for a few years before he ever met Jessica. Even then, he knew Jessica was something special. John would never cheat on Sam, and everyone knew that; even the Mafia. One of the biggest problems with the Mafia sting was John's refusal to go along with some of the guys and their escapades with women.

Jessica and John had always had what could best be described as a combative relationship. Chet had once joked they should both be locked in a room together, and both Jessica and John had turned a deep shade of red. What made things even weirder was Jessica had become best friends with Sam. While Jessica would never have done anything to break up Sam and John's marriage, once Jessica got to be friends with Sam, Jessica would have rather died than hurt Sam.

When Sam died, Trip sent his best interrogator, Jessica "The Hammer" Hammerstein into the box with John. It did not go well. John quit the FBI, told Jessica he

12

hated her, and cut off all communication to everyone, except an occasional chat with Chet.

When Jessica and Chet brought John back into the FBI, Jessica and John began to admit their feelings for each other. John knew he was crazy about Jessica; in fact, he had to admit he loved her. He wasn't about to tell Jessica that. He didn't want to seem any weirder a boyfriend than he already was. John had only ever had one girlfriend his entire life, Sam. He knew he had been acting like a fool the past couple of weeks around her, and he was determined that was going to end.

"Hey," Jessica said softly. "Did you get lost somewhere? You seem to be staring out into outer space."

"Sorry," John replied. "Just thinking." Jessica smiled and took both of his hands in hers.

Chapter 5

"Nervous?" Jessica asked with an impish smile on her face.

"Nah," John said, pulling his hand out of hers and waving it like he didn't have a care. "I mean, all I have to do is tell my former in-laws the events that lead to their daughter's death while I was slightly inebriated,"

"Slightly?" Jessica interjected, interrupting John.

"Drunk as a lord?" John asked. Jessica thought for a second and nodded. John continued. "And, I get to do it in front of my boss, my team, and, more importantly, my friends. Not to mention I get to tell everyone that I, John Fowler FBI superagent, have no clue as to the cause of my wife's death."

Jessica looked John in the eye, smirking.

"So it's like any other Tuesday?" she asked, her eyes twinkling.

John thought for a second and nodded. "Yeah, and see, that's the problem. It's Friday." Jessica leaned in close and softly kissed John. John started to kiss Jessica harder when he felt her hand on his chest pushing him away.

"Easy, cowboy," she said, looking into his eyes. "We do have an audience downstairs."

John shrugged his shoulders. "I don't care. I--" Jessica quickly put her finger on his lips. She was insistent that John not tell her he loved her until he was absolutely sure. John gently removed her finger. "Care," he said, and Jessica smiled. "For you deeply. You're the most important thing in my life right now, and I want everyone to know it." Jessica was smiling broadly. "In fact, I think I should shout it from the top of this staircase." Jessica got a concerned look on her face.

"John," she said quickly. "I don't think that's necessary."

"Oh, you're wrong, Jessica," John replied. "They need to know."

"John," Jessica said, starting to look upset. "This really isn't necessary."

"Especially since the sound carries all the way down here," Jeremiah called out.

Chapter 6

Jessica and John froze. John turned around and looked down at everyone looking up at them with an amused look on their faces. Jessica buried her head in her hands.

"And," Jeremiah continued. "If I may be so bold, I don't think there's a person here who begrudges you two finally finding happiness." Jeremiah raised his glass of ice tea toward the two. Everyone else did the same. Jessica moved her head inches from John's ear.

"You're gonna pay, Fowler, you hear me?" she asked fiercely but quietly.

"I'm not scared," John replied just as quietly while raising his glass back at them. Jessica smiled at everyone but pinched John in the back where no one could see her. John tried not to flinch.

"Get down here, and let's get started!" Arthur bellowed at John. "And just so you two know, I think Sam would be happy seeing you two together." Everyone murmured their agreement. Madeline and Rosa began to see about refreshing everyone's drinks, and the group forgot about John and Jessica for a minute. Jessica still hadn't moved from where she was.

"Maybe you should be scared," Jessica replied to their earlier conversation, quietly.

"Why?" John asked, as he turned back to face her.

"I'm not going to let you go this time," she said, looking in his eyes.

"That's good," John replied, smirking. "I don't want you to, and I don't plan on letting you go either."

Jessica looked down at the ground. John had a pretty good idea what this was about and decided to address the issue rather than ignore it. John curled his first finger and pulled her head back up to him.

"I'm going to bring up the 800 pound gorilla in the room. I was married when we met, and I would never leave her. I loved her, and I always will, but at the same time," Jessica started to say something, but John hurried on. "If I ever make that commitment to you," Jessica smiled at his ability to not use the word. "I will never leave you."

"You would for her," Jessica said matter-of-factly. John looked confused.

"She's dead, Jessica. She's not coming back. This isn't some soap opera, movie, or comic book. She's dead. Is this going to be a problem?"

Jessica shook her head no. "No, John, it's just I wasn't your first choice."

John bent down slightly and looked right into her eyes. "Listen, Sam has never made me feel like you have. I loved Sam, but Jessica, you mean the world to me. You drive me crazy, and I think I am falling into something I'm not allowed to say." Jessica pointed a finger at him and began to slowly smile at John.

"You better get down there," she said. John slightly cocked his head.

"Not until I know we're good," he replied.

"We're good," she said smiling. "I'm not calling you any pet names."

John started to walk away, paused, turned, and started to speak, grinning.

"So big baby isn't your pet name for me?" he asked.

"No, John, if I say baby, it's because you whine and cry like one," Jessica said smiling.

"As long as you hold me in your arms and comfort me," John said, his irritating grin going from ear to ear.

"Ugh," Jessica said, pretending to vomit. She pointed toward the stairs. "Go . . . . Baby." John turned and went downstairs, leaving Jessica by herself.

Chapter 7

Jessica stood there for a second, and then spoke quietly.

"I'm in your house, with your parents, with your former husband." Jessica stood there for a second and then rubbed her face with her hands. "I just want to be his first choice, Sam. Is that too much to ask?" Jessica stood there for a minute. For the past few days, both she and John had thought they had seen Sam, but they both knew it was their subconscious helping them get through the strange relationship hang-ups they both had.

"He loves you in a way he never loved me." Jessica heard the voice behind her. She looked downstairs, and no one was in the room below. They had all gone to the kitchen. Jessica really didn't want to turn around.

"I mean, seriously, you take my guy from me, and you won't even look me in the eye in my parents' own house?" Jessica spun, angry. When she turned, there was Sam, smiling from ear to ear.

"You are so easy to mess with," Sam said. Jessica chastised herself for getting angry. This was not real. It couldn't be. It had to be her subconscious, didn't it? She shook her head. It was all John's fault he had even told Jessica about seeing Sam during his first case back.

"Still trying to figure it out, huh?" Sam asked, smiling broadly. Jessica gave her a withering look, so Sam decided to change the subject. "You two really would make for a good, sappy love story. I mean, for crying out loud, it's enough to make people want to vomit."

"He chose me because you were gone, Sam, and that's not fair!" Jessica exclaimed.

Sam looked taken aback. "Well, at least we're not going to dance around what's bugging you." Sam walked toward the railing and looked down. She turned back to Jessica, smiling. "I always loved this view." Jessica was silent. Sam nodded. "Wow. You're that mad, huh? Well, you kinda won, Sweetie. You kinda won." Sam patted Jessica on the arm. Jessica had cold chills go up her spine. She had felt that. Jessica looked at Sam, questioningly. Should she ask? "Don't ask," Sam replied, as if reading her mind. "You'll stay up for nights, trying to straighten it out in your head if I told you."

Sam stood inches away from Jessica. "I can't fight you for him, Jessica, I'm dead."

"I know, Sam, and I never wanted to hurt you, but he never chose me over you . . . never," Jessica said, dejected.

"So, are you going to be all mopey and let him get away because we didn't have a duel to the death, or are you going to be happy that you're with the guy you love?" Sam asked. Sam hugged Jessica. Jessica felt the hug, making her wonder if she had gone crazy. Sam released her and walked toward her old room. She paused and turned back around.

"I'm going to tell you something that you may not want to hear, but you need to hear," Sam began. "There's a day coming soon that he is going to choose between me and you, and I want you to know that I'm rooting for you."

"What do you mean?" Jessica asked.

Sam gave Jessica an exasperated look. She walked over to Jessica and took her by the arms. Once again, Jessica knew she felt Sam's hands on her arms.

"Jessica, listen," Sam began. "He and I have had our time. That's over. It's your time with him now. You need to stand by him. You need to let him know how much he means to you. Jessica . . . . . I'm dead. If he chooses me over you, then that means . . ."

Sam let the sentence trail off. Jessica nodded and then stood for a second, thinking about what she said. "Sam, you're not just something in my mind, are you?" Jessica asked. Sam smiled, winked at Jessica, and started back down the hallway. She turned a corner and disappeared out of sight. Jessica ran down the hallway, and when she got there, Sam was gone. But she was never really there, right?

Chapter 8

John had gone in the kitchen with everyone else. He didn't tell Jessica the real reason he had been watching everyone from above. He was trying to gauge the room before he began to talk to everyone. John really wished others could see things the way he did. There were FBI experts that spent years studying human movements, postures, reactions, and other things about people. They all hated him because John just instantly knew all those things experts had spent years studying. He knew when people were lying. He didn't know what they were lying about or what the lie was, but he usually knew when people were lying. The one group of people John couldn't read were sociopaths. They had no conscience, and John couldn't put together the clues their bodies gave off with the physical evidence.

There was one case that John never was able to be any help with: the Reilly case. Peter Reilly had killed six people, and John never could get a read off of him. To John, it was like losing his sight or even his hearing. He wasn't sure what to do, and if it hadn't been for Chet and Jessica, the case never would have been solved. The two of them, and Trip, would always mention it whenever John was having trouble with a case, as a ribbing. John went along good naturedly, but at the same time, it bothered him. John wasn't a profiler, a forensic scientist, or some psychologist. John was a good old fashioned detective that was able to break cases because his mind could make connections that others couldn't see. At the end of the day, John always thought he was the easiest of the group to replace. Chet was the super tech guy, and Jessica was the greatest interrogator that John had ever seen.

What bothered John the most were some things that had been said to him about Bruce Cosby. Bruce was the Senator's son and a fellow FBI agent. Bruce was an inept agent, who had his position because someone, somewhere, thought it would make the Senator happy. The ironic thing was it didn't; Bruce's appointment went against everything the Senator believed in. Trip, Chet, and Jessica had all suggested something was off about Bruce. John had to agree; he couldn't get a read on Bruce. Bruce wasn't the first person that wasn't a sociopath that John couldn't read, but he had to admit they were few and far between. The other three believed Bruce was the killer they were looking for, partly because John couldn't read him.

John refused to believe Bruce was involved because that meant a fellow FBI agent might have had something to do with his wife's death, and that was the worst thought one could have. To think one of your fellow officers . . . . John stopped. It just wasn't something he wanted to consider, but John knew in a few minutes every piece of dirty laundry the group had would be out in public. It was time to find Sam's killer, no matter the consequences.

Chapter 9

Everyone was gathered in the kitchen. John took a deep breath and was about to begin when Arthur asked a question.

"Tell me something, John. Are you going to tell us how the current crime boss Duck rose up to power in this little tale of yours?" Arthur asked.

John smiled, thankful for the brief reprieve.

"Arthur, I have no idea how The Duck got away. For that matter, I have no idea how a low-level loanshark managed to climb the ranks to the supposed boss of the crime family. He was the one guy we had targeted that we weren't able to catch. There was one other guy we didn't get that, to this day, I still think was up to something. Ricardo Antony . . . at least, that's the name he gave me," John replied. A brief grin flashed across Trip's face. John started to ask him about it when Chet spoke up.

"You know how we said that we'd all have some stories to tell you, John?" Chet asked, looking down at his shoes the entire time he spoke. "This would be where I have to come clean." Jessica had walked behind Chet while he was talking and put her hand on his shoulder in support.

"Most of you already know I have a gambling problem," Chet said. Arthur nodded with a stern look on his face. "I borrowed some money over five years ago from The Duck. Arthur shook his head, and John winced. John looked out the window and ran his hand through his hair. He had known about the money; he just hadn't known it was Duck who had loaned Chet the money. This was not good.

"When exactly?" John asked.

"Three or four months before you went undercover, but, John, I didn't tell him until you were already undercover for a month." John blew out a breath. At least Chet wasn't the reason Duck disappeared. He gave Chet a

23

supportive smile and nodded at him to continue. "That's the part I don't understand. Let me explain it all."

"When I got behind on my payments, all he wanted to do was confirm things he had heard with me. He never got any information out of me; he just asked for confirmation," Chet explained. John looked at Chet with confusion.

"You are the only person I have ever heard of that had contact with Duck after I went undercover," John said.

Chet nodded. "I think he knew I wouldn't tell since it would cost me my job. Besides at the end of the day, I technically only borrowed money from him. I never gave away information, only nodded yes, or shook my head no. Any lawyer would have that thrown out of court."

John looked over at Trip who sat with his arms crossed. The look on Trip's face said he had heard this story before.

"That's why you've tried to keep everything in-house the past few weeks since I came back," John said to Trip. Trip looked at John and just listened. "You think there's a mole, not in the office but somewhere higher up."

Trip shook his head no. "John, I don't think there is a mole in the FBI. I think there's a mole above the FBI that reviews our cases and findings. I think the mole comes from very, very high up." Trip paused, looked at the group and shrugged as if to say, "why not". "John, I think this comes from a place we can't fight."

Chapter 10

John stood there for a second, mouth opened. He glanced at Arthur, who didn't seem shocked by the suggestion. He glanced at Jessica, who didn't look shocked either. He looked at the former Senator, and soon to be Vice-President, who suddenly was very interested in the curtains of Arthur and Madeline.

John looked over at Trip.

"I don't understand, Trip," John began. "A few days ago, you acted like you were in complete shock when you found out the former first lady may have had someone killed, but this . . . this doesn't seem to even phase you."

Trip nodded for a second. "We were talking murder then, John, not these types of political maneuvering, and honestly, I just know what I've heard rumors of in talks that I'm not allowed to tell you about." Trip paused and looked over at Jeremiah, who barely shook his head no, but it was enough for John to notice.

John walked right up to Jeremiah, who slowly turned to look at John.

"Who?" John asked.

Jeremiah tried to feign shock. "Well, why in tarnation would I know, boy?"

"Because if there is anyone who is a better judge of people than me, it's you, Jeremiah," John stated.

Jeremiah stood up and looked John right in the eye.

"Boy, there are times all you do is poke a bee's nest with a sharp stick," Jeremiah began. "You're poking more than a bee's nest this time. It's too big for you."

"Archibald?" John asked, knowing that wasn't the answer.

Jeremiah flipped and flopped for a minute.

"What is so bad that you're not telling me?" John asked.

"John," Jeremiah began gently. "Have you ever considered Sam might have died for reasons that have absolutely nothing to do with you?"

"Jeremiah, what are you saying?" John asked, beginning to make connections in his head, connections he didn't like.

"What are you saying, Jeremiah?" Madeline asked, looking very upset. "What have you been keeping from us all these years?"

"Now, now, Madeline," Jeremiah said. "I have no proof, just some thoughts, some very, very bad thoughts."

John turned back to Chet. "So Duck never wanted actual information, just confirmation?" John asked.

Chet looked back down at his shoes. John, his jaw set, walked up to Chet. Chet looked at John. Chet had tears in his eyes. John had more things clicking into place now: the look of hopelessness Chet had a few days ago and the look that something was eating Chet from inside. It all clicked with John. Not to mention that John had just had Arthur to pay off the loan owned by Archibald a few days ago.

"It wasn't Duck that owned you, was it, Chet?" John asked. "It was Archibald."

Chet nodded quietly. Trip looked away uncomfortably. Jessica kept her hand on Chet's shoulder for support. John nodded as his mind connected more pieces. "He bought out the loan, didn't he? You answered to Archibald for the last four or five years? That's why the three of you have been acting so odd. I thought it had just happened recently, but you've had Archibald holding this over your head for all of this time?"

All Chet could do was nod as the tears ran down his face.

Archibald Staples
The Staples Mansion, Virginia

Chapter 11

Tank was sitting in the kitchen of Archibald's mansion, having just finished breakfast. He loved working for Archibald. No one else fed him like this and made sure he was taken care of. This was a great life. Tank always ran the important errands for Archibald, and he was the only one allowed to carry the "red cellphone". Tank had no idea who called the "red cellphone," but whenever it rang, Tank was to alert Archibald. It didn't matter what Archibald was doing; Tank was to alert him. The phone had been relatively silent the past week. Archibald had even told Tank that he would be quite surprised if the phone rang for quite some time. That's why Tank was caught off guard when it began to ring. Tank was never to answer the phone; he was to tell Archibald it had rung.

When it went off, Tank stared at it like it was alive for just a minute and then began to run down the hallway, looking for Archibald. Archibald was in his study and could hear the 280 lb man of pure muscle running down the hallway. Tank stuck his head in the office, out of breath.

"Red cellphone?" Archibald asked. Tank nodded. "Good man," Archibald replied. Tank nodded and left. Archibald went to his safe and pulled out one of twenty burner phones. He dialed the number he had memorized. The other end picked up on the second ring.

"It's Archibald," he simply said. The voice on the other line spoke. "Well, yes, I can meet you there. I'm assuming, as the norm, you don't want silk sheets?" Archibald listened to the response and roared with laughter. "Oh, my good man, I should know better than anyone that silk can rub you the wrong way. There's days I think of getting rid of it as well. What about security? Will that be an issue?" Archibald listened for a moment and nodded. "Good, good. It will be good to see you." With that, he disconnected. Archibald opened the door and called for Tank. He handed the burner phone to Tank and simply said, "Destroy it." Tank smiled and nodded. He took the phone and began to dismember it. Archibald walked out of the glass doors of his study to his outside balcony. There, he looked out over his estate. He spoke out loud to nobody.

"I never expected you back in the game so soon. It will be nice to have someone of my equal, and dare I say even my better, to assist me." Archibald took a draw off his cigar. He did have one small worry: Bruce. Bruce had taken care of the good Dr. Freeman, and it did appear as if he was going to take out John Fowler. Archibald took another draw off the cigar and wondered how mad his daughter would be if she knew he had lied to her a few days prior. He had told her he really had nothing to do with Samantha Fowler's death, when in truth, he had quite a bit to do with it. Truth be told, if Bruce was the bullet that was fired at Sam, then Archibald was either the gun or the man holding the gun. He wasn't for sure which. He and his partner could talk tonight and figure out which one was which. Archibald smiled. Very soon, John Fowler would be out of his life, and Archibald and his partner could be back to doing what they enjoyed. He really should have had John killed four years ago, instead of Sam, but that was a minor mistake that was about to be corrected.

John
The Moores' Residence

Chapter 12

This doesn't make any sense, is all John could keep
thinking over and over. Archibald was many things, but he
was not a member of the Mafia. Why would a, then, low-
level loan shark sell out a loan to someone like Archibald?
John was trying to work things out in his head when he felt
a sharp pain in his shin that caused him to start hopping on
one foot. He looked over at Jessica who had kicked him.
Jessica had a scowl on her face and nodded over at Chet,
who was still upset. This was one of those moments John
really didn't know what to say.

"Chet," John began. Chet waved him off, snorting
out laughter in spite of himself.

"John, please don't," Chet requested. "I know you.
You'll say something that you think will help, and it will
just make things worse." Everyone in the room started to
chuckle, except John. John looked around, a little
surprised.

"Am I really that bad?" John asked.

"YES!!" The whole group chorused together as
one. Even John had to laugh at that. As the laughter died
away, Chet approached John.

"Something isn't right here, Boss," Chet simply
stated. John nodded.

"I've been thinking the same thing," John replied.
Chet turned to Arthur.

"Do you have a white board and a marker I can
use?" Chet asked. Arthur nodded and began to lead Chet
to the board in a different room.

"I don't understand, John," Trip said.

29

"Archibald fits in somewhere, but he's not Mafia," John responded. John thought for a second and then continued. "I know you, Jessica, and Chet think that Thelma's murder and possibly even Bruce fit into all of this as well." Trip and Jessica exchanged a quick glance. Both were trying to figure out what to say when John continued.

"It doesn't matter that I don't agree with you two. It may be there, and I've missed it. Everyone knows that I've missed things before. You know like--" John paused, sighed, and smiled. "Peter Riley."

Trip and Jessica both smiled. Jessica tried to cover the smile with her hand, but John had already seen it. Arthur had returned to the room, and John heard Chet fighting with the board, trying to drag it into the room. John continued with his thoughts.

"It's almost like there is a piece missing that would link everything together . . . no, two pieces. I'm pretty sure Duck is one of those pieces. From what Chet told us, he has to be. But, there is one more piece out there that would break this thing wide open." As John spoke, he carefully glanced at Arthur and the Senator. As John had finished speaking, he saw something that broke his heart. Arthur quickly glanced at Jeremiah. Jeremiah, so quickly and so slightly that it wouldn't have been noticed unless you were looking for it, shook his head no. John instantly knew what he had seen. Arthur knew that Jeremiah knew something, and Jeremiah was refusing to share it. John didn't know why, but if Jeremiah Cosby was holding back secrets, then it must be for a very good reason. The kind of reasons that were from, how did Trip put it, the kind of place that he couldn't fight. John decided to let what he saw go for the time being. He hoped once he painted the full picture that Jeremiah would feel like he needed to talk about what was going on, but if not . . . if not, John was prepared to get Jessica alone with Jeremiah. This was ending, if it killed

John. All the secrets were going to be exposed, and John was going to find Sam's killer.

Chapter 13

Chet was rolling the white board into the room. He felt a little uneasy. While he knew John didn't blame him for Sam's death, he had to wonder if he unknowingly had something to do with it. He had heard John talking about the missing piece, and in his gut, Chet knew he was right. Many times John had said Chet looked for conspiracy theories everywhere, but this time, Chet thought he was really onto something.

Chet placed the board where everyone could see it and pulled out a marker. He thought the best thing to do was to start a timeline and fill in the gaps as they went. He started at the top with John returning to the FBI, and at the bottom, he put twenty-five years ago, Veronica Staples. John looked at the bottom of the board and then to Chet.

"It's the first time that we know of Archibald and his daughter Veronica," Chet said. John nodded and turned toward Rosa.

"You didn't ever know her as Veronica did you, Rosa?" John asked. Rosa shook her head.

"The only time I ever heard her called Veronica was those last days I was employed by Mr. Staples when she returned," Rosa replied. "In fact, she was referred to as Silk by Mr. Staples for the past little bit."

John cocked his head at that. He turned to Trip. "That was her secret service code name, wasn't it?"

"Yes, it was," Trip replied. "I mean, this is all very interesting, but what does this have to do with anything?" Trip stood up as he was talking. He had been leaning on the arm of a couch before. Trip felt like he was missing something. There was that look again on John's face. The look that said he had found something. No one knew what, but John had found something. John turned to Trip.

"Why would you refer to your daughter by her secret service handle?" John asked. Trip shrugged.

"John, I know you're trying to pin things on Archibald, but that link, that's pretty thin," Trip replied. John grinned. Jessica groaned inwardly and rolled her eyes. Here he goes, she thought.

"We've caught bigger with thinner," John replied and began to turn away.

"Have we?" Trip asked. John stopped midway and turned back to Trip. Every eye was on Trip, and a deafening silence fell over the room.

"Have we ever caught a case bigger than this, John?" Trip asked. John knew what he was asking.

"Are you telling me this is bigger than the Mafia case, Trip?" John asked. Trip shrugged.

"Bigger as in the number of busts? No. Bigger as in the power and standing of the people involved, I honestly don't know, John. It feels like it, though," Trip replied. John pinched his bottom lip as he listened. "We need to approach this like it's the biggest case we've ever seen." Jeremiah harrumphed. Everyone turned to look at him. Jeremiah looked directly at John.

"Boy," the future Vice-President began. "It doesn't matter how you approach it. This is too big for you." He looked around the room. "It's too big for all of you." John looked at Trip, who simply shrugged his shoulders and then nodded in agreement with Jeremiah.

Chapter 14

"What do you know?" Jessica demanded from Jeremiah. Jeremiah just looked at Jessica, shook his head, and remained quiet.

"What he probably knows is something he's always suspected. A few days ago, he could have told us everything he has ever suspected, but now, he has been sworn to secrecy." Trip said. Everyone turned to look at Trip, except John. John was slowly nodding.

"Because he's about to be the Vice-President of the United States," John said. Trip nodded. "He's seen files and been told things that he can't share with us, or anyone else." Jeremiah sat there, stoic. Jessica got up, walked over to where he was seated, sat down beside him, and put her arm around him.

"It's alright, Jeremiah. We know you wouldn't keep anything from us if you didn't have to," she said. Jeremiah shifted in his seat. Jessica took her arm from around his shoulders, not wanting to make him uncomfortable.

"It's not like I want to," he began quietly.

"He'll tell us what we need to know," John said, with a twinkle in his eyes. Jeremiah snapped his head around towards John.

"Boy!! You wouldn't dare!!" he exploded. Jessica was trying to hold in her laughter, but couldn't help it and snorted. This caught Jeremiah, and everyone else in the room off guard. Jessica was laughing out loud now.

"Jeremiah," she said between laughs. "You might as well ask him not to breathe than to not do what he does."

"I don't think this situation is quite as funny as you do, young lady," Jeremiah said, trying to keep his dignity. John's face was red, trying to hold in the laughter.

"Jeremiah," John began. "I just need you to confirm what you can. I don't want you to tell anything that would violate national security." Arthur and Madeline

34

looked at each other with that statement and then at John, confused.

"What else could it be?" John asked as an answer to their unasked question. "Jeremiah Cosby would only keep something from the public, or outright lie, for the greater good." Trip nodded his agreement.

"We've all known Jeremiah for a long time," Trip added. "If he's not telling us something, it's got to be for a very, very good reason." Arthur looked at Jeremiah. Jeremiah was looking down at his hands.

"Arthur," John began. "Whatever you think he knows, let it go."

Arthur sighed. Jeremiah looked at Arthur, and Arthur nodded. John decided it was time to turn this hunt back to the right direction. He turned back to Rosa.

"Rosa, who was Archibald talking to when he referred to his daughter as Silk?" John asked. Rosa shrugged.

"I don't know, Mr. Fowler," Rosa replied. John looked at Rosa. Rosa smiled. "I'm sorry . . . John." John smiled at her. "The strange thing is, I know when Mr. Staples is talking to Duck, and it's like he was talking to him, but better."

John looked at her quizzically. "What do you mean?" he asked.

"Mr. Staples talked to his people like they were dogs. Or, he talked to people like he didn't respect them. There are a few who work for him that he talks to like normal people, but for the most part, you know Mr. Staples knows he is better than they are, and he doesn't hide that. But, this man he talks to when he refers to her as Silk, he respects him." She paused. John was hanging on every word. That was probably why he hadn't noticed that Jeremiah had shut his eyes and began to clutch his stomach like he was sick. Rosa continued. "This man-- Mr. Staples either thinks of him as an equal, or," Rosa paused and then continued like she couldn't believe what she was saying. "Mr. Staples thinks this man is better than himself."

With that, Jeremiah jumped up and ran to the bathroom. John heard the door close and then heard the unmistakable sounds of Jeremiah retching. John looked at Trip, who looked down at the ground. Trip swallowed, looked back at John and mouthed two words, "Too big." He didn't say anything else and just shook his head.

David George
Virginia, Parts Unknown

Chapter 15

David awoke with a start and listened. He thought he had heard one of the many alarms he had rigged up around the abandoned shack he was living in go off. He rolled out of bed and crept over to the window. He remained perfectly still, looking for any signs of movement. He saw none, but that didn't mean anything. David army crawled to the back of the room where he had built an escape hatch, opened it, and crawled into the space under the structure. He exited under the back of the shack and slipped into the woods. He made a long circle around the perimeter, checking each of his alarms. After he was sure none had been tripped, he relaxed. David knew he was too tense, but right now, he didn't care. He was planning his big move.

David returned to the shack and began to go over his plans again. He had guard schedules, blueprints of the house, and diagrams of all perimeter security for the Staples mansion and land.

David began to check his gear, ending with the sniper rifle. Where Bruce had gotten the rifle from, David didn't care. Bruce, pretending to be John, had freed David from a psychiatric hospital. Bruce gave David an address to a weapons locker. When David opened it, he was stunned to find the rifle that was made by the manufacturer that had recorded the world's longest sniper shot at over 2,700 yards. David wasn't the marksman the record holder was, but he was a great shot. He found several places slightly over 300 yards that would make a perfect nest for him to set up.

David smiled as he held the rifle. Very soon, he was either going to see Veronica in jail or in a wooden box. He had his preference, but either one would work.

"Veronica, you better hope John, or someone, arrests you soon, because if they don't . . . I'm going to finish this."

The Moore Residence
Virginia

Chapter 16

After Jeremiah's exit, everyone was up milling about, trying to make sense of what they had all learned so far. Madeline and Arthur came over to Chet, who was standing close to Trip. Neither of the men were speaking.

"I don't understand, Chet," Arthur began. "How did what happened to you have anything to do with my daughter?" Chet looked at Trip. Trip nodded, and Chet spoke.

"Arthur," Chet began. "After I missed a payment, Duck told me how I could make things right without losing any fingers, or my life." Arthur frowned. While he thought Chet had messed up, he didn't want to see anyone hurt. Chet continued. "He told me that all I had to do was verify a few things with Archibald. He said that it wouldn't be anything illegal, and at first, it wasn't." Chet sighed and looked at the floor; when he looked back at Arthur, there were tears in his eyes. "It's like Duck disappeared, and Archibald took over everything on the collecting end. Since money was never exchanged and we never got anything on tape, it was always my word versus his. In fact, the requests had all but ended by the time John came back to the FBI. There was only one request when John came back, and that was to bring back John. After hearing everything, I can only assume that Archibald wanted John back to either save his daughter or see how well what happened in Kentucky years ago was covered up. Heck, maybe it was both."

"Or it could be to see if any of what happened all of those years ago could be connected back to him," Arthur offered.

Chet thought for a second and nodded. "That's true."

"So let me get this straight," Arthur began. "You are worried that something you may have told Archibald might have led to Sam's death?" Chet nodded. "Son, not to rain on your parade, but I really don't think you did anything or said anything that would have caused my daughter's death." Chet looked a little relieved. He turned toward Madeline, took a deep breath, and began to address her.

"Madeline, if what I did ever caused--" Chet began. Madeline cut him off.

"Chet, I don't blame you, Arthur doesn't blame you, and I'm sure Sam would never have blamed you," Madeline said gently. "If you think you owe my daughter something, then may I suggest that you let go of all of this self-doubt, and use your superior computer skills to help us solve this crime."

Chet nodded. He felt a huge weight lift off his shoulders, like he had finally been absolved of his sins. Chet had an idea. He excused himself and went to find John.

"I've thought of something," Chet told John.

"Well let's hear it then, boy," Jeremiah Cosby said, as he entered the room. "This whole thing about killing and government conspiracies is making me sick to my stomach, literally. The sooner we're done with it, the sooner we'll all feel better."

John nodded. He thought about the wording Jeremiah had just used: government conspiracies. No one had said that except for Jeremiah, and he was the one person in the room with the highest standing in the government. The person with the second highest standing had kept saying this was all too big. John didn't like where this was leading. The simple answer was Veronica Staples, but that didn't feel right to John. No, what felt right made

John's skin crawl. He had to have more proof than just his gut instincts. John's biggest fear was what he thought Jeremiah might know. If John was right, the discussion itself was not making Jeremiah ill. It was the knowledge of things that the rest would never know due to national security. John didn't know exactly what the former Senator knew, but he was sure it was the clue they all needed to break this case wide open.

Chapter 17

Chet went back to his whiteboard.

"Here's what we know," he began. "In December of 2005, word came down from Quantico to begin an operation to bring down the alleged members of the Mafia in New York City." Chet paused and looked over at Trip to verify. Trip nodded, and Chet wrote it down on the whiteboard.

"In March of 2006, Edward Gates was murdered while under FBI protection," Chet continued while writing the information on the whiteboard.

"Was that the case you were telling me about the other night at the diner, John?" Arthur asked.

"Yeah," John replied. "For anyone who doesn't know, I had nothing to do with the Gates case. I was contacted by Quantico," John paused and looked at Trip for help and confirmation. Trip rubbed his head a second, thinking.

"The best I can figure, the call came from them no more than 10 minutes after they learned of the murder," Trip said. John nodded and turned back to the group.

"Quantico asked me to take the hit on this one. They wanted me to look like it was possible I was dirty. I was told all along that I would be cleared in the end, but this was the chance the FBI wanted to take to get someone deep into the Mafia."

John paused and looked around the room. Jessica had her arms crossed, looking more than slightly irritated. John started to think. Did he ever tell Jessica the whole story about the Gates case and him going undercover in the Mafia? He couldn't remember, but from the look on her face, he was pretty sure he didn't.

"So, I wasn't crazy," Jessica said. John wasn't fast enough to stop a smile forming on his face from that statement. Jessica gave him what John had always referred to as the stink eye.

"You know what I mean," she admonished him. "Your basketball team was playing the night the assassination happened." John smiled and looked down at the floor. "They were in, what did you call it, the quarterfinals for the national championship?"

"The excellent eight?" Chet asked. John groaned. Jeremiah snickered.

"Tarnation, son, none of us ever thought you did what the FBI accused you of," Jeremiah stated. Arthur turned away, his face slightly reddening.

"It's alright, Arthur," John said. Madeline looked at Arthur and backhanded him on the shoulder. Arthur shouted out and rubbed his arm. John chuckled. "My story was supposed to be as questionable as possible. That was my way into the Mafia." John looked down, then back at the group with tears in his eyes. "It was actually Mark Glass that got me in." John looked over at Trip. Trip shook his head and bit his bottom lip.

"May I?" Trip asked. John nodded.

"John was working undercover after finally being accepted by the Mafia. John believes he was the reason that Glass died." Trip began. "Glass had been undercover for years, but he never had enough clout in the bureau, or wasn't important enough for the Mafia. Because of that, he couldn't get deep enough inside the Mafia. He was too far outside their inner circle to really hurt the Mafia, and I think they kept him outside the inner circle for a reason." Trip paused. Arthur was watching Chet and Jessica. Arthur had heard this story a few nights ago at the diner. Chet was shaking his head, and Jessica had a slight frown on her face. Trip continued.

"John was suspended for a while. He was told the best thing to do was be visible to them and to seem like he was upset with the FBI. So, during the suspension John started to spend time at a local Mafia dive. He sat, drank, and told stories about how the FBI had screwed him over and how he wanted to get even with them. That's when he was eventually approached." Trip paused and turned toward John. "The name of the place, what was it?"

"This Thing of Ours," John replied. Jessica looked at John like he was crazy.

Chapter 18

"Are you serious?" Jessica asked. John nodded, chuckling.

"Oh yeah," Trip replied, smiling slightly and nodding. "The owner thought it would be funny. Anyway, many made men decided to hang out there." Trip looked over at Madeline. "Made men are those who have taken the blood oath of the Cosa Nostra."

Madeline gave Trip a withering look.

"I watched the show, Trip," Madeline replied. "I know all about the Mafia." Trip smiled and held his hands up in defense. Jessica looked over to Madeline and gave her an encouraging nod and smile. Trip continued.

"Anyway, John would sit in the bar all day, drinking, waiting on Mark to show up with other Mafia members." Trip paused a second and looked at John. John nodded. "I . . ." Trip stopped. John had been waiting for this. Trip had never handled what happened to Mark well. John had to admit he hadn't handled it well himself. John walked over to Trip and patted him on the shoulder.

"I've got this, Trip," John said softly. "I mean, it's my fault and the FBI's fault he's dead." Jessica and Chet both shot forward in their seats. The Senator looked down at the floor. Arthur looked away, having heard the story a little while before. Rosa and Madeline both looked very confused. John sighed and began.

"What the higher-ups claimed to never know--" Both Trip and Jeremiah shot a quick look at John at his choice of words. John filed that internally and continued never missing a beat. "Was Mark was suspected of being a mole. I was being introduced, and the members thought I was the real thing: an agent who couldn't take any more of the politics of the FBI and was ready to take care of myself, by any means necessary." John paused and looked down. He spoke softly.

"It was at the Mafia trials that took place after the busts, that I found out that the order had been out to kill Mark for a few weeks for being considered a rat." John paused for a second. "I don't know if that's right or not, the rat part. I'm not for sure if you can be considered a rat by the Mafia if you're not a made member."

While John was going on about Mark being a rat, Jessica looked over at Trip, who was stunned.

"How did you know that?" Jessica asked John. "You were nowhere to be seen when it came to anything to do with the FBI for almost four years? That trial was a year and a half ago!"

"Remember the bum you asked to be thrown out of the courtroom?" John asked.

"Of course I do," Jessica replied. "Gah! He was repugnant! He smelled like a distil . . . wait, that was you!?!?"

Chapter 19

Jessica was stunned. She took a few seconds to regain her senses enough to question John. "You said you hadn't drank since Sam's funeral!"

"I haven't," John replied. "I have poured some pretty cheap whiskey over myself though, and then bathed myself down with that body spray stuff." John paused for a second, thinking. "They should put suggested usage labels on those things."

"Where did you get that beard?" Jessica asked, still amazed. "That thing was horrific. It looked like a rat's nest. It makes sense now that it was a disguise. It was the worst fake beard I have ever seen!" John pursed his lips and nodded. Jessica looked confused for just a second, and then, John rubbed his jaw. Jessica realized at that point the beard had been real and that she had just stuck her foot and part of her leg in her mouth. She clasped her hands together at her pinkies and covered her mouth with her fingers. She tried not to laugh into her hands, but failed. John nodded, taking the ribbing good-naturedly.

"So," he began. "The beard doesn't do it for you, huh?"

Jessica shook her head and took her hands off her face.

"No, Baby, not so much," she replied, her eyes twinkling.

"Baby?" He mouthed. Jessica shut her eyes when she realized what she had said and who she had said it in front of.

"If I might," interjected Trip. "I don't think in the middle of the story of how a FBI agent was killed is the best time for you two to have a romantic break."

John nodded once, his lips pursed together. Jessica sat back in her seat with her head down and her hand over her eyebrows as if to hide from the embarrassment.

"Anyway," John continued. "Apparently, several of the guys, some made and some not, didn't care for Mark. We were at the bar I mentioned earlier. There were two places I was to meet them at: the bar and a strip club called The Daily Grind. After I had a talk with the boss, Anthony Lucciano, and I told him I was a married man and took my vows seriously, I was allowed to meet them at the bar." John paused, thinking.

"Is that why they called you Saint?" Jessica asked. John smiled and nodded. Jessica turned to Madeline. "Apparently, some of the guys used to have big fun with the girls that worked at the strip bar, and John refused to. It actually got him respect from the head of the family." John continued with the story.

"There was some drinking going on. Well, there was a lot of drinking going on. I didn't catch everything that was said, or what exactly that led to it. All I know is an argument broke out, Mark fired off one of his zingers at a guy. The guy got upset, pulled his weapon, then shot Mark. Mark died instantly. He didn't bleed out, or anything like that. It was quick. By the time I crossed the room to him, he was dead. It was all I could do to keep my cover. In fact, I was scared to death that I was next. It was only the thought that they might kill Sam as well that helped me keep my head on straight." John paused for a minute and then continued softly.

"I think this might have been my lowest point. I was told to cover everything up," he paused with tears in his eyes. "I was an FBI agent, and so was Mark. I could make this all go away they thought. I made it out to be an accidental shooting. I told the FBI that Mark and I had been out drinking, and he had too much. I told them he had pulled his gun on some people, and the guy, thinking he and others around him were in danger, shot Mark. Chet helped me out on this one. I had him go back and make the murder weapon registered. I falsified records and lied

48

about the death of an FBI agent." John paused again and looked down at the floor while he gathered himself.

"This was probably my test, and never did the Mafia think an agent undercover would do what they asked, but I did. I was in." John turned to where he could see both Jeremiah and Trip.

"You know, even now, I find the orders from the top strange," John said. "We had enough at that moment to take down 85% of the men on the list. We had enough to bring down the boss and cripple the organization. We had enough to put them away for a long time. That wasn't good enough for someone, though. Whoever gave the order wanted everyone, and I mean everyone . . . except Duck. I mean they obviously didn't because once it showed up in my reports that I had no intel on him, I was told to not pursue him." Trip looked disgusted, and Jeremiah looked like he wanted to throw up again. John began to stare at Jeremiah. Jeremiah wouldn't meet John's glance. John spoke very quietly.

"What exactly did you mean when you said earlier that Sam may have died for reasons that had nothing to do with me? Why would anyone have anything against Sam?" Jeremiah refused to look at him. John continued. "I mean, you know better than anyone she never did anything wrong in her life. Heck, some even think she's really your daughter. She was so upstanding; her entire life's work was to help kids. It was like, since we didn't have any, she had to help every child she could! She was the most caring person I have ever met. She put up with my crap for years! How can you think it had to do with anyone but me?" As John was grilling Jeremiah, Jessica happened to glance at Madeline and Arthur. She wasn't John when it came to reading people, but she could tell something was wrong. When John mentioned kids, Jessica saw the looks on Madeline and Arthur's faces, and for the first time in her life, she thought she knew how John felt when something clicked into place, and he didn't want it to.

Chapter 20

Arthur noticed Jessica watching him and Madeline and shook his head no at Jessica. His eyes were pleading with her to ignore what she had seen, but she couldn't.

"No," Jessica whispered as she shook her head. It wasn't defiance; it was shock and disbelief. John and the Senator both turned to watch Jessica. The entire room was staring at Jessica. Arthur had tears forming in his eyes. Madeline just held Arthur's hand.

"John," Jeremiah said. "If you won't ask what's going on with Arthur and Madeline, I'll tell you everything. I'll resign from my Vice-President's office, and I'll tell you everything I know." Everyone slowly turned and looked at Jeremiah except Jessica and John who were staring at Madeline and Arthur.

"Will it tell me exactly who killed Sam? More importantly, can I figure it out myself if I keep this investigation going?" John asked.

Jeremiah didn't answer. Madeline looked at John and gave a sad smile. John looked at Jessica. Jessica felt John's gaze but wouldn't return it.

"John, please," Jeremiah begged. Arthur shook his head and forced a smile.

"I guess this is what happens when someone tells you to solve a case no matter what," Arthur said, tears streaming down his cheeks. "Sam always told me you'd follow every lead, no matter how uncomfortable it was to you, or the suspect." John nodded and gathered himself. He knew what he needed to do.

"When?" John asked as gently as possible.

"John, don't," Arthur pleaded softly. John shook his head with tears in his eyes.

"Before me?" John asked quietly. Trip's mouth slowly opened as it dawned on him exactly what they were talking about. Arthur nodded slightly. John nodded and turned away to talk to Jeremiah.

Jessica looked at him in amazement.

"You're really going to let this go?" she asked.

"If it was before me . . . I told you what someone does before I'm involved with them is their business. How hypocritical would it be of me to question them about it?"

"John," Jessica said forcefully, "it might be a lead." John realized he was going to lose the argument and the staring match.

"It wasn't her fault," Arthur said quietly. John whipped his head around toward Arthur and Madeline.

"Arthur," Jeremiah said softly.

"It's not your fault, Jeremiah," Arthur responded. John looked over at Jeremiah who stood up. He straightened his suit and looked John right in the eye.

"I'ma sorry, John," Jeremiah began. "I'ma goin' to give you two choices here. I can come 100% clean, which means I then have to resign from the Vice-President's position. It won't be enough to help you completely solve your case; that I surely know. The other option is I can come 90% clean and give you a trail you'va not even considered. I have no idea if it will lead to the killer or not, but it will be worth your time reviewing."

Madeline looked at Jeremiah.

"You don't think?" Madeline simply asked. Jeremiah shook his head.

"I don't know, ma'dear," he replied. "What I do know is I'va had it with the world thinking that boy is the saint he is." Trip nodded in the corner. John raised an eyebrow at him.

"Et tu, Brute?" John asked. Jessica rolled her eyes. Trip shrugged and answered.

"Take the deal for 90 percent, John," he began. "I'm willing to bet we can figure the other 10 percent out."

Chet wrote down Mark Glass on the white board and circled it. John looked at him questioningly. Chet shrugged.

"You can't resist a mystery," Chet replied. "You're going to hear the Senator out, but I don't want you to lose your place about the mob. I still think all of this fits into one big picture."

John nodded and looked over at Trip.

"Too big a picture?" John asked. Trip looked at the board, and then John. He smiled and answered.

"For the first time since we started this, I'm beginning to think no," he replied.

Bruce Cosby 3 Days Ago
Abandoned House

Chapter 21

Bruce walked into the abandoned building, headed down to the basement, and sat down in a chair. He looked over at his captive. The bag was still over his captive's head. Bruce liked it down here. It was very, very cool down in the basement; some would say cold. He felt at ease in the dark cold place. He was sure if Dr. Freeman was still alive, that would mean something to him. Bruce chuckled and elbowed the captive.

"He's not, though," said Bruce, laughing. "I killed him!" Bruce broke out in a fit of laughter. Bruce had been enjoying himself way too much the past few days. He had thought about killing so many people over the years, but he had only cut loose the past four years or so. In fact, if you took Sam out of the picture, all of the killings had happened over the past few weeks. Bruce elbowed his captive again.

"I did take her out of the picture!!" Bruce roared with laughter. He felt so free right now. Somewhere in his mind, he knew he had to get himself under control. Once John was dead, he couldn't kill anymore. He was sure all of the murders would be pinned on John if he did everything by the plan. He went over to a desk in the room and grabbed a notebook. Bruce had written everything in his secret language that only he could see. Bruce looked over the notebook and studied it. He smiled while he went through his plan, piece by piece. He looked over at his captive when he finished.

"You want to read it, don't you?" Bruce asked. Bruce thought for a minute and decided it would be ok. It wasn't like his captive was going to get loose anytime soon. Bruce walked over and held the notebook up in front of the captive's head. Bruce stood there a second and started to get angry.

"You can't see it, can you?" Bruce asked angrily. "I know, I know. I don't know what's wrong with me." Bruce threw his head back and laughed. "I can't believe I left the bag over your head!" Bruce reached down and pulled the bag off the dead man's head. Ricardo Antony looked, and smelled, like he had been dead for a few days; it had actually been ten days.

"Whew!" Bruce exclaimed as he waved the putrid smell away. "You're getting a little ripe! I'm not going to be able to hide you down here much longer!" Bruce looked around the room and sighed. "Oh well, I guess it's time to move on." Bruce laid down the notebook that was opened on the blank page that only he could read. He began to gather up everything he wanted to take, paused, looked back at the dead man, and came and sat down beside him.

"I think it's time you and I had a good heart to heart talk before I start this," Bruce shook his head. "I'm sorry Ricardo, but once I light the match on this place, there's no turning back, and we won't be able to have these good talks anymore."

Chapter 22

Bruce looked around the basement. He found the irony of where he was if no one else did.

"Listen, Ricardo," he began. "I'm going to do something that's brilliant. We're here in Edward Gates's old home. You know, he was the witness against the Mafia that was killed under FBI protection, and John took the blame for it. I'm going to blow this place up with you in it. I'm sorry about having to torture you like I did, but I have to make the police think that the Mafia took you out. I've put this note in your pocket that reads, 'where the rat was found.'" Bruce began to giggle uncontrollably.

"The great thing is, the FBI and police will think we're talking about you and Gates. When, in truth, and it will take a while because John is stupid, I'm talking about where you and John met. You know that bar, This Thing of Ours. It's going to be great! That's where I'll kill him! I'll make the FBI think John's gone off the reservation and been killing everyone that had to do with his wife. Dr. Freeman, that woman in Virginia that Trip knew, you, the hooker that John used to know back when she worked at the strip club, all of them will be pinned on John. I'm going to tell everyone that John confessed to me that he killed his wife in a drunken rage and set the apartment to explode. I'll go to daddy and tell him to bring in an outside team to investigate the whole thing. I'll make sure Archibald handpicks the team. Once he sees I'm not a liability, he'll gladly come around. I mean, it's not many that have my skill set." Bruce paused and thought. He looked at the decaying corpse. "I'm going to need you to keep quiet about me letting David George loose. He won't like that at all. Oh darn." Bruce looked up in alarm and then at the remains of Ricardo. "I'm going to have to go kill that girl, the one that saw me the night I impersonated John."

Bruce got up and started to walk around. He thought for a few minutes, suddenly stopped, and smiled. If a snake could smile, that would resemble the smile on Bruce's face.

"I know what I'll do," Bruce said as he walked over to the corpse and slapped its leg. The pants made a funny noise, and Bruce looked down disgustedly.

"I'm doing you a favor, burning you up," Bruce said, laughing. He gathered his things and headed out into the night. He got several blocks away and made a phone call that set the timer on an incendiary device in the house he had just left. He smiled and kept walking until he reached the fleabag hotel he had rented under an assumed name in cash. No one was paying attention to him; no one there wanted to be known or recognized, so no one looked him in the face. Bruce headed out to the back parking lot.

"It's too easy," Bruce said quietly to no one as he got into the stolen car and headed toward the psychiatric hospital he had broken David George out of. It was the last mess to clean up before the grand finale between John and him.

The Moores' Residence
Virginia

Chapter 23

Everyone agreed to take a break before Jeremiah told his story. Jessica pulled John away from everyone to have a private conversation.

"John," Jessica began. She seemed to be struggling with what to say to him. "How are you holding up?" John bobbed his from head side to side, grinning.

"I'm fine, so far," he replied. "I think the question is, how am I going to be after I hear this?" Jessica nodded, but looked concerned.

"John, she loved you," Jessica said. John smiled and looked back out toward the main room. He didn't see anyone gathering yet. He thought for a second and looked back at Jessica with a sad smile on his face.

"The part of me that talked to you about what someone does before they are in a relationship with me knows that," John began. "The part of me that wants to strangle the part of me I just described knows that." John paused and looked around the room just trying to collect himself. He continued. "It's not a question of love, but a question of why she never told me. There's only a couple of reasons I can think of, and . . ." John trailed off.

"John," Jessica began. "What do you think happened?" John looked at Jessica like she lost her mind. She stared at him, insistent. John ran his hand through his hair and started to speak several times, but each time, he saw the look on her face and stopped.

"Say it," she said forcefully.

"She had a child and didn't trust me enough to tell me," John said quietly. "She didn't think I could handle it." John looked down and spoke barely in a whisper. "She thought I'd leave her." Jessica cupped a finger and raised John's head. His gaze met Jessica's withering look.

"Listen, you big idiot," Jessica said, very vexed. "Have you ever stopped for a second and considered it did not have a single thing to do with you?" From the look on John's face, it was apparent that he hadn't. "Mr. Detective, she thought she couldn't have kids, she worked with kids, and she was the first one to go buy someone a baby shower gift." John still wasn't connecting the dots. Jessica gave an exasperated sigh. "Maybe something happened that she wasn't comfortable talking about?" John still looked confused. Jessica grabbed John by both ears. "She might have lost the baby, you doof!" Jessica let go of his ears, and John started rubbing them. He began to think through their entire relationship where it came to kids. When they couldn't have kids, Sam had always told John it wasn't him, even though he kept insisting he needed to be tested to rule it out. John quit rubbing his ears and began to press against the middle of his head with the middle two fingers of his right hand and slowly rubbed them back and forth. He had goofed, and big time.

"You really need to work on that," Jessica said, a little snarly as she crossed her arms. John lowered his arm from rubbing his head and looked at her with a pained expression on his face. Jessica continued. "This world doesn't revolve around you, John Fowler, no matter how great a detective you are."

She turned to walk away.

"You forgot to mention how it does because of my charm!" John called after her. Jessica made a, "phfft," noise with her mouth and kept walking. "My rugged good looks?" he called. Jessica ignored him, went upstairs into Sam's old room, looked around, picked up one of the stuffed animals on the bed, and sat down.

Chapter 24

"You're behind me, aren't you?" Jessica asked. When there was no answer, she turned to look. There was no one behind her. Jessica sighed, turned around, saw Sam, and threw the animal in surprise. Sam laughed, walked over, and sat down on the bed beside her. Jessica felt the bed shift under her. Sam smiled, shook her head, and leaned in toward Jessica as if to tell her a secret.

"You're not crazy," Sam said quietly. She picked up the animal Jessica had tossed and held it. Jessica looked at it and then at Sam. Sam grinned broadly.

"Why didn't you tell me?" Jessica simply asked. Sam looked at the animal and then at Sam.

"If I did, we would have cried, ate some ice cream, and then, we would have both had to keep a secret from John," she replied. Sam looked back down at the animal; her eyes were getting wet. "It's the only secret I ever managed to keep from him. Thank God his social skills are so poor that I never had to directly avoid any questions." Jessica was replaying Sam's first statement in her head.

"Sam, why would we need to keep it from John?" Jessica asked.

"I'm not going to be able to see you anymore," Sam said quietly. "I want you two to be careful." Sam looked Jessica directly in the eye. "I want you two to be as happy as humanly possible. You two deserve to be happy."

"Sam," Jessica began. "Who killed you?" Sam looked back down at the animal, sighed, and a single tear fell on the carpet.

"Jessica, it's not the question of who killed me that you need to ask; it's the why and who had someone kill me," Sam answered. Jessica looked down at the floor as she ran that statement through her head. She found herself staring at the wet spot in the carpet that had come from Sam's tear. She looked back to Sam, but she was gone, and so was any impression in the bed. The stuffed animal was back to where it was supposed to be. Jessica stared back down at the wet spot on the floor to make sure she wasn't hallucinating. She stood up, took a look back at the bed, and turned to leave the room when Sam grabbed her in a hug.

"I'm rooting for you, Jessica," Sam whispered in her ear.

"Sam, are you an angel?" Jessica asked. Sam pulled back from the hug. She placed her hands on her friend's shoulders and smiled.

"If I was, do you think I would be allowed to tell you?" Sam asked. Jessica smiled. "I think we did promise that if one of us died first, that one would look after the other," Sam gently reminded Jessica. Sam rubbed Jessica's shoulders and then removed her hands.

"You're about to disappear again, aren't you?" Jessica asked. Sam crinkled her nose and nodded. Jessica looked down, and when she looked back up, Sam was gone. Jessica looked back at the tear spot on the floor and it had either dried up, or was never there. Jessica shook her head. It had to be her head playing tricks on her. Jessica walked out of the room.

Sam stood in her room, watching her friend leave. She knew this was the last time they could see her like this. The next time she saw them . . . Sam sighed. She knew John would figure out who killed her. She just didn't know if he would figure out everything, and if it would kill him in the process.

Chapter 25

Jessica walked back down to the main room where everyone was gathered. She saw John sitting on a loveseat by himself. She sat down beside him, still a little bothered by what she had seen a few seconds ago. It had to be her mind. It had to be. John was looking at her, concern on his face. Jessica smiled and took his hand. She wasn't for sure what Jeremiah was about to tell them, but she was sure it was going to be hard on John. Jeremiah looked over at Madeline and Arthur. Arthur nodded for Jeremiah to begin. He spoke very softly when he started.

"Well, let's see here," Jeremiah began. "It was over 20 years ago." Arthur nodded, Madeline held up three fingers. "23?" Jeremiah asked, and Madeline nodded. "Well, you would know better than I," Jeremiah responded. "While I don't know the exact time nor date, I never will forget that evening as long as this ole boy shall have the grace to walk on this earth. It all started with what I thought was going to be a splendid time. It was a dinner party at my home. Many rich and powerful people were there, most of whom I despised, you must understand, but there are necessary evils one must deal with when running for elected office in this great land."

Jeremiah took a breath and tried to continue when Madeline got up, walked over, and hugged him. She pointed at the couch, and Jeremiah went and sat down without a word. She smiled at him and then looked at everyone in the room. She took a deep breath and continued the story.

"You have to understand," she began. "There are certain things expected of us." She made a sweeping gesture at Jeremiah and Arthur. "There are many people we know that we can't stand, that we are expected to be seen with, whether we want to or not." Tears formed on Madeline's cheeks, but her voice remained strong. "Archibald and his family were there, as well as Veronica's soon-to-be husband, Kenneth Nichols, and his family. Everyone who was anyone was there. It was either Jeremiah's first or second re-election campaign. Somewhere during the night, Samantha disappeared." Madeline turned toward John and looked right at him. "Even then, we knew she was to be trusted, so we thought nothing of it." John nodded. "We looked around for her when we got ready to leave and couldn't find her. Now, you have to understand, these parties drag out sometimes, and the children would leave. I trusted her, John. I knew she wouldn't do anything." John nodded again, his heart breaking watching Madeline. "The staff was known to take the children home sometimes, and we called home to see if she was there. She was already tucked into bed. This was around 2 a.m. I hadn't seen her for nearly 6 hours." Arthur looked sick to his stomach, and Jeremiah didn't look much better. "Don't you understand what we're saying? John, one of Arthur's servants said he took her home a little after 10 p.m. We don't really know what time she got home." John was looking sick. Madeline was looking at him, tears flowing freely from her eyes. "John, we didn't believe her. Heaven help me, we didn't believe her."

Chapter 26

John looked at Madeline, confused. There were many things his brain could process and make connections on, but this . . . this was one of those things Sam had always said he just wasn't wired to handle. Madeline looked at John and knew he didn't understand what she was saying. John felt an arm go around him; it was Jessica. She didn't know what to say to John, but she knew, just like Madeline, that he didn't understand. Jessica nodded at Madeline to continue.

"She woke up the next morning and told me she felt uncomfortable and sore," Madeline continued. Trip really looked uncomfortable. "I asked her if anything had happened last night that I should know about. Sam laughed at me, and then, her look turned serious. She said she couldn't remember what happened after we had separated at the party. I thought nothing of it, and she didn't seem to at the time. Looking back, I think maybe I missed something. I think she suspected then but couldn't bring herself to face what had happened."

Madeline had tears freely falling down her face. Jessica watched John's face. It was a confused mess. Jessica knew it was starting to dawn on John what was going on, but either his mind didn't want to believe what was being said, or couldn't. Madeline gave John a sad smile. She knew he hadn't yet come to grips, or understood, what she was saying. She walked over and sat on a foot stool right in front of him, taking his hands into hers.

"I need you to listen to me, John," she said. John nodded. "About six weeks or so later, she missed her monthly cycle. She told me she was concerned. I think she had figured out by that time what had happened. You know Sam. When something went wrong, she didn't go to pieces. She just dealt with it. Do you remember that about her, John?" John nodded, still confused. Madeline looked over at Jessica. "Did you know?" Madeline asked Jessica. Jessica shook her head no.

"Thinking back to some of our talks, I think she was trying to tell me," Jessica responded. "Did she ever tell anyone outside of the family?" Madeline shook her head no. John was starting to get the idea, but he couldn't believe it. Tears were forming in his eyes. Jessica had her arm around his shoulders. Arthur spoke in a broken voice.

"We did her wrong, John," he said. "We should have believed her when she told us she didn't know who the father was." John was shaking his head no. Jessica turned John's face towards her and spoke softly.

"John," Jessica began, as tears freely flowed down Madeline's face. "Someone took advantage of Sam. John, someone raped her and got her pregnant." John had only felt like this once in his life, the night Sam died. This time, instead of having to grill him about his wife's death, Jessica held him. Arthur came over to the three, while Chet, Rosa, Jeremiah, and Trip left the room without a sound.

Chapter 27

"He may be the greatest detective in the world, but when it comes to matters involving his family or ones he loves, that boy is blinder than a bat," Jeremiah said. The four had gone into the kitchen to leave the family to deal with John. Rosa shook her head.

"What's wrong with him?" she asked. Chet shook his head and looked at Trip. Trip and Jeremiah shared a glance. Jeremiah ran his hand through his white hair and blew air into his cheeks, searching for answers. Finally, he nodded at Trip. Trip faced Rosa and chose his words carefully.

"I'm going to say this the only way I know how," Trip began. "His mind just isn't wired like yours or mine." Rosa tilted her head and looked at Trip with confusion. Trip sighed, stuck his hands in his pockets and continued. "John can make connections in his mind. He can see the way things are supposed to fit, but to use some of Sam's words, he sees things cleanly. When John gets involved with emotion--once again, Sam's words here--it gets muddled for him. He can't make the connections. He can't understand things the way that normal people can."

"That's weird," Rosa responded. Jeremiah barked a laugh, Chet laughed into his hand, and Trip smiled broadly. Chet started thinking about something and turned toward the other two.

"Is that why he's having such a hard time with Sam's case?" Chet asked. Trip nodded. "Is that also why he can't see that Bruce may be dirty? Is it the fact that Bruce is in law enforcement and in John's world . . . well, you just don't do that?"

"In John's case, I don't think it's just that Bruce is in law enforcement, but also that he knows him," Trip replied. "Think about the soldier David George. John didn't have a problem with him, and I think it's because he knew things about David George, the person, before he

66

found out he served in the armed forces. John knows Bruce as only a FBI agent, and that's all he can see. As for Sam . . . he has to do the same thing he did with Mark Glass. He has to depersonalize the case."

Chet looked confused. Trip looked down and spoke softly.

"In that case, he drank," Trip said. He raised his head and looked at the group. "He drank until he became an alcoholic. I really don't think John was an alcoholic until Mark was killed. I don't know that for sure, but that's what I think. He was able to numb the connection to Mark with alcohol to let his brain do what it needed to do. The kicker was, there was no real case to solve. He was just gathering evidence. He wasn't digging, finding leads, following cold clues to the ends of the earth, solving a big mystery, or anything like he normally does. He was just gathering evidence."

Chet looked very confused. Trip glanced quickly at Jeremiah, who just barely shook his head no.

"Then, why was John sent undercover?" Chet asked. "I mean, it seems like a complete waste to send a great investigative mind to do something other than investigate, especially with John's lack of social graces. Or was that part of it? Did the Bureau think that John's lack of social charm made it more likely that he was ostracized from the FBI?" Jeremiah closed his eyes. Trip put his hands back in his pockets. He looked down at the ground. After a second, his head snapped back up with anger on his face.

"I don't know for sure, Chet," Trip answered. "But I swear, if I didn't know better, someone was trying to have John killed." Chet's face was covered in shock, as was Rosa's. Jeremiah's expression never changed; he just patted Trip on the shoulder.

Chapter 28

Trip refused to say anything else, and the four made their way back into the living room. John gave a sad smile to the four as they entered. Arthur had gone back over to his seat on the couch while Jessica and Madeline stayed with John.

"It's really not necessary," John said to the two. "I mean this isn't about me, right?" John was looking at Jessica when he asked the question. Jessica beamed at him. John smiled back. "I mean, it's honestly not about me, but I am going to murder whoever did this to her."

"Careful, agent," Jessica said, still smiling. "You just admitted conspiracy to commit murder to an FBI agent."

"I think he'll be cleared of any charges," Trip said. Everyone slowly turned and looked at Trip. He waved his hand at them. "Don't you people start with me. You know I'm hip deep in this mess with you." John nodded, stood up, and walked over to Trip, his hand extended.

"I always said you were too worried about the rules to uphold the law," John said to Trip. "I was wrong, and I am sorry." Trip was taken aback. He reached out and shook John's hand.

"John," Trip began. "I should apologize to you; it's my fault about Sam." Tears were forming in Trip's eyes. "She came to me thinking she was being followed, and I blew it off. She thought someone was watching her to dig up dirt on you. She was worried you had been made. She spotted someone watching her days before she died. I put someone out there to watch you, but I didn't protect her." John stepped back. Trip prepared for the verbal barrage. Chet and Jessica both jumped to Trip's defense.

"It wasn't his fault, boss, you know I should have watched out for her since you were undercover," Chet interjected.

68

"No, John, she was my friend," Jessica insisted. "I should have been watching her." John watched the three argue whose fault it was, smiling.

"This?" John asked. "This is the big dark secret you three have been trying to keep from me?" John laughed and the three turned toward him, irritated. "I mean, really, this is it?!? Sam goes to you because she thinks someone was following her and you think I'm going to go postal on you?"

"If we had done something more, she wouldn't be dead!" Jessica insisted. The other two nodded their agreement.

"Or one of you could be dead as well," John said quietly. By the expression on their faces, it was obvious the three of them had never considered that possibility. "You didn't kill Sam, and I didn't kill Sam, but it's time we find out who did." John turned, and went back to his seat in front of Madeline. The others took their former positions in the room. "Madeline, if you could, would you continue your story?" John asked. Madeline nodded.

Chapter 29

"There was a fight," Madeline began. Arthur shook his head and put his hand over his eyebrows as if to hide from the shame. "That's probably not the right term. Arthur and I both got quite upset, and Sam calmly told us that she hadn't done anything with anyone."

Madeline blew out a breath and smiled.

"She said regardless of what had happened, it was time to find out if she was pregnant. She told us that she was going to raise the baby if she was." Madeline looked at John who snorted a laugh. Jessica smiled and rubbed John's shoulders.

"That was Sam," Jessica said quietly. "She never cared how someone got into a predicament, only what needed to be done next." Jessica paused for a second and asked the question that had never really been answered. "Did she lose the child? I only ask because I don't see her giving the baby up for adoption." Madeline smiled.

"I'm getting there," she answered. Jessica nodded. Madeline continued. "It's hard to admit when your teenager is right, but Arthur and I took her to Dr. Nichols." John's head snapped up with that detail. Madeline nodded. "Yes, it was Brian Nichols, the current President's father." Madeline looked at Jeremiah and remembered the events of the past few days. "I guess that's not right. He's the soon-to-be former President, correct?" Jeremiah nodded, and Madeline continued. "He said everything was fine, and there was no sign of any problems. She was about six weeks along. Arthur and I took Sam out of school and hired a private tutor for her." John glanced quickly at Jessica who was looking at him.

Both of them were thinking of Sam's famous tirades on parents being embarrassed by their kids and how a parent should always put their child first, regardless of how uncomfortable the situations made the parents. They quickly looked back at Madeline, but she had seen the quick glance.

"I'm guessing you've heard Sam's displeasure over that decision?" Madeline asked.

John squirmed. "Not directly," he answered truthfully, but evasively.

"I can hear her now," Arthur said. Everyone turned toward him. It was obvious by his actions he had been ashamed of the way he had acted years ago. "You've done nothing wrong, Dad. I've really done nothing wrong, but you don't believe me. That's not the point, though. What happened, happened to me, and it has nothing to do with you. Whether you or society can see that is not my fault, but you are taking it out on me whether you want to or not." He stopped and took a second to reflect on the moment all those years ago. The look on Arthur's face spoke of how proud he was of his daughter. "I wish I had half the character she did."

"Arthur," Jeremiah began. "You'va admitted you made a bad decision then, and now you're doing everything in your power to right a wrong. What more could any man ask for?"

Arthur looked shocked. Everyone knew the uneasy history between Arthur and Jeremiah. Jeremiah and Madeline had once been an item. After they broke up, Arthur and Madeline dated for a brief time and then were married. For years, many believed Sam was actually Madeline and Jeremiah's daughter. For Jeremiah to say what he said spoke volumes. Arthur spoke very quietly. "Thank you, Jeremiah. Thank you."

Chapter 30

The room had gone quiet for a few seconds with everyone thinking about Sam. Madeline finally broke the silence with the remainder of the story.

"To make a long story short," Madeline began. "Sam went into labor just like she was supposed to. Everything had gone perfectly fine in the pregnancy. We never knew anything was wrong until the doctor came out of delivery and told us the baby was stillborn. There had been complications during the birth, and Sam had been put under. Something went wrong . . ." Madeline stopped to gather herself. She took a deep breath and continued. "We were in such shock that Dr. Nichols took care of most of the arrangements of the burial for us," Madeline paused, and John thought she was finished. She took a second to gather herself and continued quietly. "Sam named her." John looked up from his thoughts. Madeline was looking directly at him. John knew the child's name.

"Amanda?" John asked. Madeline nodded, a little surprised. John smiled. "She always loved that name," he explained. "Anytime a child by that name was brought in to her, it always seemed she did a little more with that child than the others." John stopped and shook his head. "She gave 120% to every child that came in, but . . . blast." John put his head in his hands. "This is one of those times I need her to help me." Jessica put her arm around his shoulders.

"We know what you mean," Jessica said. John pulled his head up and took her hand.

"How quickly can we get an exhumation order?" He asked. Jessica shook her head.

"John, we can't do that," she replied.

"Why not?" He asked. "Virginia has no statute of limitations on rape or sexual assault!"

"We don't know she was raped," Jessica said gently.

72

"She was under 18!" John responded.

"We don't know the age of the boy," she replied. "Besides, who do you want to compare samples with?" John blew out a breath. He looked over to Trip for help. Trip was shaking his head no and even mouthed no to him.

"Sam didn't want that done," Arthur said quietly. "I said the same thing to Sam years ago, John, but she didn't want it. She just wanted to move on."

John wanted to argue, but he knew better. His mind was slowly working. He was trying to approach this as a mystery, not as an act of violence against his wife. He kept reminding himself that this happened before he knew her, hoping that would allow his mind to work. Only one question kept surfacing in his head. He knew it was improper, and they would all want him to be delicate in this situation, but he didn't know if that was possible. He had known himself too long to ignore the thought.

"Do any of you think that whoever raped her might have killed her?" John asked as gently as he could. Jessica's head jumped back like she had been slapped. Trip covered his eyes with his hand and withheld a groan. John looked at Madeline helplessly; she nodded it was ok. John continued. "I don't say it to be insensitive, but you have to admit, if someone committed that act of violation against her and got away with it, it is possible that same person escalated the violence against her. Given what you told me, Trip, about someone following her, isn't it possible?" Trip looked uncomfortable but nodded reluctantly.

"I've never wondered, John," Madeline replied honestly. John looked at Arthur.

"It never occurred to me," Arthur replied. John nodded. He didn't know if the two cases were related, but there was nothing saying they weren't. In his head, he felt the lock tumbling. John had a bad feeling the cases were related, and he knew he needed a DNA sample from the child to prove it.

Undisclosed Location
Archibald Staples

Chapter 31

Archibald walked into the waiting area of a small room inside a restaurant. One of the men inside held up his hand. Archibald smiled and stuck out his arms to be frisked.

"Sorry, sir," said the man who was frisking him. "You know the rules."

"Of course," Archibald replied. "How has he been?"

The man looked back at the table where the gentleman Archibald had been referring to was sitting. He looked back at Archibald and gave a slight shake of his head.

"He's taking it as well as can be expected," the man replied. "You know Kenneth; he takes everything in stride." The man looked like he wanted to say more but held his tongue. Archibald smiled.

"It's ok. Go ahead," Archibald urged.

"I think part of him is happy to be divorced," the man replied, waiting for an explosion out of Archibald that didn't come.

"You've been around a long time," Archibald began. "I think we all know that his marriage was a power arrangement." The man nodded. "The good thing is, now that he's leaving, he and I can meet more often."

"I think he'd like that, Archibald," the man replied. He shook his head for a second and snorted a laugh. "He has a much better relationship with you than her." Archibald laughed out loud at that remark.

"And I with him," Archibald replied, clapping the man on the shoulder as he entered the room. Archibald smiled. Here was his equal, if not his better. Archibald had recognized his friend's ability at a very young age. Truth be told, they were more like father and son than father-in-law and son-in-law. Archibald watched as the man who started out being his protégée, rose from the table and approached Archibald to give him a hug.

"Archibald," his former protégée said. "It is so good to see you." He and Archibald shared a hug. Archibald backed up, still having his arms around the man.

"Kenneth," Archibald began. "I am so sorry for what my daughter did."

"Are you ok with my choice?" the man asked, and the two men released each other.

"Do you mean the divorce, or resigning as the President of the United States of America?" Archibald asked.

"Both," Kenneth Nichols admitted.

"I understand why you had to resign, to protect the three of us," Archibald began. "But, did you have to send her back to me?" Kenneth roared with laughter.

"That was her idea," Kenneth said through fits of laughter. "According to her, I never was as great a man as Daddy was."

"That girl's a fool!" Archibald hissed. Kenneth extended his hand toward the table as the two men sat to begin their meeting, a meeting that would forever change the life of John Fowler.

Chapter 32

The two men ordered lunch. They ate and exchanged stories and other small talk. Kenneth sat back while his dessert, cheesecake with strawberries on top, was being served, thinking of the best way to express his problems to Archibald. Archibald was grinning

"Am I that obvious?" Kenneth asked.

"Only because I have known you for so long," Archibald replied. "Just tell me, Kenneth." Kenneth grinned at his old friend.

"John Fowler," Kenneth simply said. Archibald chuckled.

"You've never been very happy with him," Archibald said, leaning back and lighting a cigar.

"He took what was mine," Kenneth replied. "If I had known how things would have to play out, I never would have agreed for him not to die when he was undercover. Oh, well, we must agree our friend came out best in that deal, and it has served us all well. It's a shame he was ever on the radar to start with. I've always worried that might come back to haunt us. You know how he follows a lead like some dog following a scent." Archibald nodded, thought, and then spoke.

"You had already gotten what you wanted out of that several years earlier," Archibald countered. Kenneth smiled. "As for our friend, he provides us with what we need without anyone finding out we're connected." Archibald paused and smiled. "Besides, we both know it took all of my powers of persuasion and our friend's to keep you from killing John. You really hate that man." Kenneth nodded.

"While I do appreciate the trophy you provided for me, that girl did fascinate me," Kenneth reflected. A smile crossed his face. The smile would have made most men's blood run cold. Kenneth continued. "I think the same reason I was so attracted to her is the same reason she couldn't be mine." Archibald raised his eyebrows questioningly. "Take my current bride." Archibald chuckled, and Kenneth grinned at him. He continued. "We both have our own agenda, but at the end of the day, we take care of each other. Well . . . at least we did." Archibald grinned broadly. "Tell me, Archibald," Kenneth continued. "Did she ever actually have the affair with the agent?" Archibald took a long drag off his cigar and looked at his friend.

"Would it have mattered if she did?" Archibald asked. Kenneth roared with laughter. Archibald joined him. When both men calmed to a chuckle, Archibald continued. "I warned you years ago that her secret could end things badly for you one day." Kenneth nodded.

"That you did, old friend," Kenneth replied. "That you did." Archibald studied Kenneth for a second.

"The agent did not sleep with your wife," Archibald said quietly as he took another drag off the cigar.

"That's good," Kenneth replied. "Otherwise, I'd have to kill Bruce since he killed the agent, and you know how I love to get my hands dirty." Both men roared with laughter with that last statement.

Chapter 33

After both men stopped laughing, Kenneth finished his dessert and had a cigar of his own. After a few minutes of comfortable silence, Kenneth spoke.

"What of our other friend?" he asked. Archibald once again took a long draw off his cigar before he answered.

"He has backed away from us by my request," Archibald answered. "I don't think Fowler could connect the pieces, but he ferreted out Veronica's secret." Archibald gave a slight shrug with his last statement. "We may have a small problem," Archibald said with a slight frown on his face.

"Bruce," Kenneth replied. Archibald nodded. Kenneth sighed, placed his elbows on the table, and pressed his hands together where his index fingers touched his upper lip. He nodded at Archibald to continue.

"He's gone rogue," Archibald began. Kenneth chuckled lightly. Archibald grinned broadly at his friend. "You know I never had the opportunity to compliment you on using him the first time. What you suggested to him . . . well, you took care of all problems that could be traced back to you."

Kenneth grinned and brought his hands down to where his right hand was making a fist, and his left hand was covering it. He leaned forward a second. "Let's be honest. Early on, my father managed to hide some of the evidence, and then, you gave me the opportunity to hide the rest. For that, I will be ever grateful."

Archibald smiled. "Kenneth, there is one thing that has always remained constant about you ever since I've known you. Regardless of your age, size, position in life, or any other obstacle, whatever you want, you get . . . and if you can't . . . ." Archibald's smile was very evil. He continued. "You make sure no one else can have it. It has been my privilege to help you at a young age, and I have no

78

problem saying you have surpassed my every expectation. I couldn't be more proud of you if you were my own son." Kenneth nodded his head in acceptance.

"As for Bruce," Archibald continued. "He's worse than normal." Kenneth raised an eyebrow. "My sources tell me he has killed several and is running around planning to finish off Fowler." Archibald looked away for a second, slightly irritated. "He seems to have freed David George. The authorities aren't aware of this yet, but someone, supposedly John Fowler, placed him under federal custody." Kenneth shook his head.

"Is she in any jeopardy?" he quietly asked. Archibald shrugged and studied Kenneth. "He will try to kill her." Archibald nodded. "Are you prepared to lose her?" Archibald looked away for a moment and then back at Kenneth.

"She is becoming a problem," Archibald answered. Kenneth nodded. "She has no more value to our plans." Kenneth nodded again. "I don't wish her death," Archibald began but stopped.

"Nor do I," Kenneth gently added. "But we've all had to make sacrifices." Archibald nodded. "Then, it is agreed?" Archibald nodded. "Only if it comes to it," Kenneth added. "After all, there's no need for loss of life when it's not warranted," Kenneth said as he lifted his glass. Archibald lifted his, and they toasted. Two of the three members of their cabal were together, and all was beginning to seem right to Archibald again. With Kenneth out of the White House, they could work more closely together. He would hate to lose Veronica, but if that was necessary, then he would sacrifice his little girl. After all, Kenneth had sacrificed the one he wanted to be with more than anything to reach his goal. And, as for the other person close to Kenneth, well, she was turning out to be an even greater asset than Veronica ever was. If it came to it, Veronica would be sacrificed. After all, the three agreed they would do whatever necessary to get what they wanted. Archibald felt on top of the world, and soon, very soon, he thought John Fowler would be gone from this world.

Psychiatric Hospital 2 Days Ago
Pamela Davis

Chapter 34

Pamela's shift was just ending as the sun was shining through the window of the front doors of the hospital. It always came right over the desk and hit her right in the eyes. Pamela was so tired. She had been studying for her tests, and working the graveyard shift was about to take its toll on her. Her replacement came in, and Pamela informed her of what little had happened the night before. After she finished, she stumbled out to her car and began the five minute drive home. As she got to her home, she thought about how great it was she lived a couple of miles off the main road. To top that off, the driveway was very long, and her house was surrounded by trees. She thought of the great sleep she was about to get in her blacked out room in the back of the house. The best thing was she didn't have school or work for the next three days. Pamela smiled as she entered the house and began shedding clothes. She jumped into her bed and was out in seconds. Within minutes, she was sound asleep and never heard the light footsteps that were coming to her room.

Bruce looked at the nearly lifeless form in the nearly dark room.

"Oh well," he said quietly to himself as he picked up a throw pillow. "I guess we'll just do this one old school." Bruce walked over to the bed and began to smother Pamela. There was little struggle, and within a few minutes, Bruce decided to check on her. She was dead. Bruce smiled, laid the pillow over her face.

"Sorry" he said to the dead body. "Ok, ok. So I'm not." Bruce cocked his head to the side and looked at her. "You should probably thank me," he continued. "Once

81

they figured out that it's your fault a nut like David George went free, they would have fired you." Bruce was very proud of himself. He went back down to the basement to check the charges he had planted. Once he was satisfied with their countdown, he headed out of the house through the woods in the back where the victim's ATV was located. He rode the ATV through the woods until he came to a little dirt road where his vehicle was located. Bruce got in the car and headed back toward New York City. It was time to begin the show and send John on his wild goose chase. Things were very close to ending . . . one way or another.

The Moores' Residence
Virginia

Chapter 35

John wasn't happy. He knew that he needed to have the child excavated, but he had absolutely no proof that it was the right thing to do. He knew if he had a few minutes with Chet, he could get Chet to agree, but everyone else . . . that just wasn't happening. John decided as cold as it was, this was getting him nowhere. It was time to go back to the story of Mark Glass and the Mafia . . . but first.

"Jessica," John began as he turned toward her. "You said something a second ago that bothers me." Jessica stiffened. She glanced over at Trip and Chet. Chet was looking away on purpose, and Trip set his jaw. She slowly turned toward John with what she hoped was a smile on her face. "What do you mean if you had done more?" Jessica feigned confusion. "The word more implies you did something. What was that something?"

"John, if I didn't know better, I would think you're getting back at your girlfriend for grilling you in the box all those years ago," Trip said. John turned toward Trip. John did a dance inside. It was Trip who he thought had done something. John thought if he questioned Jessica or Chet, Trip would jump in. He was right.

"Ok, Trip, then how about you answer the question?" John asked, smiling.

"Happy?" Trip replied, looking from Jessica to Chet. John raised an eyebrow. "Oh, come on, John, you know in the end these two really had your back and convinced me to do something. I had you followed." John started thinking about his time with the Mafia and when Sam was worried about someone following her. "It was Ricardo Antony." John's head snapped around so he could look at Trip. Trip was smiling. "You didn't get that one did you, Mr. Detective?"

"Are you serious?" John asked in a low voice. Of everything he had heard today, this shook him up the most. John had been convinced for four years that Ricardo had something to do with Sam's death. The biggest lead he had in Sam's death had just been snatched away from him.

"I know you thought he killed Sam," Trip said very quietly. "I couldn't tell you when you were a murder suspect, and then, you quit the FBI. I couldn't very well tell you when you first came back, and then, you wouldn't take her case. What was I supposed to do, John?" John shook his head and waved Trip off. John got up and walked over to the window and looked out. Jessica started to go to him, but Jeremiah stopped her.

"Let me talk to him, ma'dear," Jeremiah said. Jessica nodded, and Jeremiah walked over to John. "Nothing like thinking you know every dadblasted thing there is to know and having the carpet yanked out from under you is there, my boy?" John turned toward the Senator, shock still on his face. Jeremiah nodded. "I wonder if you would've known all of this, if you would've come back to the FBI sooner?" John looked at Jeremiah questioningly. It was something he had never thought of. He bobbed his head around, thinking. He blew out a sigh and slowly nodded.

"Yeah, probably," he admitted.

"I don't understand why, my boy," Jeremiah stated.

"I never had proof," John replied.

"Proof?"

"Jeremiah, I have the case files I made and kept on every person who I thought had something to do with Sam's death. I never had anything on Ricardo that proved he was guilty," John admitted.

"That's because he doesn't exist, son," Jeremiah said to a confused John. Jeremiah grinned. "I now know why Trip enjoys messing with you when he can." John smiled. "Ricardo Antony is a fake identity for an undercover police officer." John slowly closed his eyes. He started to chuckle. When he opened his eyes, everyone was looking at him like he was slightly crazy.

"Of course," John said, with relief on his face. "That's why I could never find out anything about him. Part of my time as a private investigator I spent trying to investigate Ricardo, but he was like a ghost. He just didn't exist." John looked over at the group. "It's time you guys told me everything about him." Trip nodded, and Jeremiah and John headed back to the group.

Chapter 36

"I guess I need to start at the beginning," Trip began. "After Sam came to me, I tried to pull you off the case. You were drinking heavily. It was obvious to everyone that what happened to Mark had affected you. I was afraid you were going to go in there one day and just kill everyone in that bar." Trip paused, remembering how John was at that time. He continued. "When that didn't work, I made a call to the local police department to see if there was anyone undercover who could help us out. There was; all I was given was his undercover handle. I never asked for more."

"So, you know?" John asked quietly. Trip nodded. Everyone looked confused, especially Chet and Jessica. Trip held his hand up to stop any questions.

"I'll get to it," he said. "I told him where you were supposed to be, and he found you." John was looking away. Jessica was concerned. "John, no one is upset." John snorted and continued to look away. Trip shook his head and continued. "The reason John is upset is what happened the night before the big bust. After gathering the last of the information that John needed to bring down everyone and finding out about a gathering, John stayed behind at the bar after everyone left." Trip waited for John to say something, but he remained quiet. Trip continued; his voice very low.

"Ricardo was given a bartending job, thanks to a little arm twisting. The owner thought the overthrow of the Mafia would save his business, but he was wrong. Anyway, it was closing time, and John was the only one left. Ricardo locked up the bar with John inside and tried to talk to him." Trip paused again, waiting for John to say anything, but he still remained quiet. Trip continued.

"John . . . snapped." Jessica looked at John, who was still was looking away. "He had been undercover so long, holding in everything about Mark's death. I honestly feared that he was about to commit suicide in that bar. I thought he'd go in one day and go out in a blaze of glory. I thought he was going to kill every one of them he could, and the rest would be arrested for killing him." Trip stopped. He was on the verge of becoming very emotional. He had always been accused of not caring about his agents when nothing was further from the truth. What had happened to Mark, John, and Sam had changed Trip. To this day, Trip believed if he had been more involved, Mark never would have been in the position he was that got himself killed.

"It was my fault," John said, softly interrupting Trip. "We let this go on for months after Mark's death. I should have arrested everyone right there when Mark was killed, but that's not the point. They were testing me, and the test was to get me to cover up Mark's death." Jessica put her arms around his shoulders.

"John, we got them all in the end," Trip said, trying to reason with him.

"I blew my cover at the most crucial point," John fired back.

"You were under too long and burnt out!!" Trip roared. Everyone jumped back. "They were setting you up!" John's head snapped up. He sprang up and got right in Trip's face. Trip was furious with himself. He had gone too far.

"Who? Say it, Trip," John said quietly.

"I can't prove it," Trip replied just as quietly.

"Just say it."

"Archibald," Trip said just above a whisper. "Somehow, Archibald had his hands in this, and I can't prove it."

Chapter 37

Jeremiah put his cane between the two and slowly pushed John away. John backed away, smiling.

"You're in on this, too, aren't you, Jeremiah," John said with his cocky grin back. Jeremiah shook his head, refusing to answer.

"What does he have on you two?" John asked.

"He doesn't have anything on me," Trip replied calmly. "I just can't find out who he owns high up."

"How does he own them? Duck?" Jeremiah shut his eyes. Trip put his hands on his hips and sized up John.

"Are you sure you're ready for this question?" Trip asked. John looked dumbfounded.

"If I'm not now, I'm never gonna be, Trip," he replied.

"I think so, but I don't think he owns them. That was the wrong word. I think they're all in it together." John stared at Trip like he had a second head growing out of his neck. They both turned as one to look at the Senator. Jeremiah looked like he wanted to be anywhere other than where he was right then. Jessica got up, walked over to Jeremiah, put her right hand on his left shoulder, and with her left hand rubbed his arm.

"This isn't proper," Jeremiah tried to complain with little in his voice to support the complaint. He sighed and nodded confirmation. He turned, pulling away from Jessica and went to sit down. John was doing a dance internally. Now, he had something. Jeremiah was never going to tell them who, but he had confirmed a suspicion, and now, they had somewhere to look. John thought he knew where, but he didn't think anyone was ready for that yet; well, maybe Trip knew and was ready, but the rest sure weren't.

Chet started looking at his board. He was disappointed that nothing was jumping off it. John walked over and held out his hand. Chet handed him the maker.

On the side, John wrote Archibald, Duck, and mystery man.

"This is your evil empire folks," John said, turning toward everyone. "For some reason, these men needed or wanted Sam dead. I don't believe any of these men actually killed Sam, but they had her killed. I am going after them with everything I have. I can't ask anyone to help me, but I promise you I'm going to figure out this entire thing."

"I'm game," Chet piped up. John smiled at his friend.

"Someone's got to keep you in line," Jessica chorused in. John turned toward her, smiling.

"I'll give you all the support, whether it be financing or moral support, you need," Arthur joined in with Madeline sitting beside him, nodding.

"I'll do what I can," Jeremiah said quietly. John smiled at the Senator and his in-laws.

"I'm in it to the end, although it might be the end of us," Trip said wearily. John had to agree with him.

"Then, the next question is how does Duck figure in to all of this?" John said. Chet reached over and took the marker from John.

"I think I know this one," Chet answered, surprising the room.

Chapter 38

Bruce checked his watch. He had a little over 24 hours before the three devices he had planted, exploded. He was a little concerned about the one at Pamela's house. He had to do that one manually, and he was afraid it would be off a few seconds one way or another with the explosion. Oh well, as his father said, "All you can do, is all you can do, and all you can do is enough." He really hated that saying and his father, but Bruce had resigned a long time ago all you could do was play the hand you were dealt in life. He burst out in laughter with that last thought. Oh, he couldn't wait to see the look on Daddy's face when he killed John Fowler. Bruce paused for a second. Since Sam was his illegitimate sister, would that make John his brother-in-law? Bruce thought for a second and decided he would hate John more if he was his brother-in-law. Bruce nodded. It was decided. John was his brother-in-law. Bruce just wished he could break John's neck the way he did Sam's.

Bruce walked through the building, giving it a once over. After he was done, he was satisfied. The bottle he had taken from John and Sam's apartment the night he removed his illegitimate sister from the earth was in place. The electricity was working like he needed it to. Bruce was ready. He left the bar and headed to his temporary home. In a little over 24 hours, he would finish what he started four years ago. He knew Archibald would be upset that he didn't ask for permission, but Archibald had other things to worry about, like David George.

Now (23 hours later)
The Moores'

Chapter 39

Chet wasn't used to all the eyes being on him unless he was giving information from a computer. What he was about to tell everyone were things he had learned while working for Archibald. He took a deep breath, steadied himself, and began.

"You all know that I confirmed information for Archibald and Duck," Chet began. He looked over at Jessica who gave him an encouraging smile. "What you don't know about Archibald is a fascination he has with the old school Mafia."

This piqued John's curiosity. "How old school?" He asked Chet.

"Charlie Lucky Luciano old school," Chet replied. John gave a low whistle in surprise. He was very interested in that information. John knew quite a bit about Luciano himself. When he went undercover, he knew he needed to brush up on his Mafia history. Chet continued. "I don't know how much you know about Lucky Luciano or the legend of him. Luciano set up what is referred to by many scholars as The Commission. Basically, it was the governing board of all Mafia families in the United States. The Commission was formed after the murder of Salvatore Maranzano in 1931. Maranzano had taken over the Mafia, after Joe "The Boss" Masseria was killed in April of 1931 at one of his favorite restaurants while dining with Luciano. The legend says Luciano excused himself to go to the restroom when several men rushed in and shot Masseria to death." Chet looked around and saw everyone was fascinated with the story. He continued.

"In September of 1931, Luciano and others were upset with Maranzano. Maranzano had figured out that others were mad at him and wanted him dead, but not before it was too late for him. Maranzano was actually planning on having Luciano and the other men killed. However, he was murdered by four hired men. Luciano is the man that supposedly arranged the killing. Luciano ran the Commission until he was imprisoned in 1936. During his time in charge, Lucky made some tough calls. There was a mobster named Dutch Schultz that questioned the Commission's authority when he wanted Thomas Dewey murdered."

"Governor of New York, Thomas Dewey?" Jessica asked, surprised. Chet nodded.

"The very same one," he replied. "The Commission turned on Schultz and had him killed in 1935. They also used Murder Inc. in 1935 to take out anyone who didn't go along with their plans. Anyone who stood up against the Commission found themselves dead, quickly." John had been processing all of this, and things were starting to fall into place. Chet saw John's face and grinned broadly. "John, would you like to explain what you figured out to the rest of the class?" John leaned back and shook his head no.

"You're running it nicely," John replied. "It looks like, for once, you found the conspiracy, my friend."

"If you don't mind," Jessica said, looking perturbed. "Would you let the rest of us in on it?"

"Don't you see, my dear?" Jeremiah asked quietly. Jessica turned toward Jeremiah and noticed Trip was rubbing his brow, looking uncomfortable. "Chet thinks the same thing that many of us do. Archibald and his cronies have created a new Commission."

Chapter 40

Jessica stared at Jeremiah for a second, then Trip, and then she turned to John. John was sitting there slowly, nodding his head.

"You think someone high up is a part of this Commission?" John asked Trip and Jeremiah. Trip looked at John and then over at Jeremiah. Jeremiah pursed his lips and nodded. Trip looked over at John and raised his eyebrows as if to say, there you go.

"I'd call it more a cabal than the Commission," Chet interjected. John thought for a second and nodded. The rest of the room looked slightly confused. Chet thought for a second and then began to explain.

"The Commission is said to still be in place today within the Mafia," Chet explained. "What we're dealing with is the Commission with a twist. Regardless of what was done over the years, everyone involved in the original Commission was a made man. We know that Archibald Staples is many things, but he is not Cosa Nostra. Archibald has a deep respect for the Commission, but namely Lucky Luciano."

"Out of curiosity," John interjected. "Is there any connection between Lucky Luciano and the Lucciano Crime Family run by Robert the Duck Mariotti, Jr.?" Chet smiled.

"Duck would like you to think there is," he replied. John nodded. That made a lot of sense. Many made men got where they were because of who they were related to. Jessica's brow furrowed. "Something wrong, Jessica?" Chet asked.

"Wasn't Duck supposed to be one of the ones you were supposed to find evidence on to arrest during your time undercover?" Jessica asked John. John smiled and nodded. Jessica looked even more confused. John looked at Chet, who looked as excited as a 5-year-old boy at

Christmas. John held his hand open to Chet to signal for him to continue.

"Don't you see?" Chet asked, all giddy. "Duck knew what was coming from the FBI by way of Archibald, so he got out of town and had nothing to do with the Mafia during John's investigation. They are part one and part two of this group that are looking out for their own well-being. The third person is the one that Jeremiah and Trip keep inferring exists, which would be our third member of this cabal."

"You keep saying cabal . . ." Jessica said, her thoughts trailing off from confusion.

"I'm sorry," Chet began. "A cabal is usually a group of people who are out for their own self-interest. The word derives from Kabbalah from the Hebrew scripture. It usually refers to occult doctrine or secrets, and I think we can all agree this whole thing has been shrouded in secrets."

"Chet," Jessica began. "Are you saying there are at least three men who are yanking the strings on most major things that happen in the United States?"

"I don't think so," Chet replied. "I think they are only concerned about a certain area. I'm not for sure how big. I don't know if it goes just from DC to New York City or not, but I think the entire U.S. is too much for just these three. Now, if there were more members we don't know about . . ." Chet trailed off. The next voice they heard surprised them all.

"I think it's just the eastern seaboard," Rosa said very quietly. They all turned toward Rosa when she began speaking. She looked very nervous. John nodded at her to continue. "I think it goes all the way from New York City to Florida."

Chapter 41

John let out a low whistle at that revelation. He looked over at Trip who looked over at Jeremiah. Jeremiah didn't look like he was trying to hide anything this time. He looked as genuinely surprised as the rest of them.

"Washington, D.C., and New York City is bad enough," the Senator began. "But, if they control things all the way down this great country's eastern seaboard, then Lord have mercy on our souls! This thing runs even deeper than I dared to imagine. Trip, we have to do something!" Trip looked at the soon-to-be Vice President and nodded.

"You cannot stop them," Rosa said quietly. John turned toward her. She seemed very nervous.

"Why do you say that, Rosa?" he asked.

"Mr. Archibald, he's dangerous," she said simply. "He makes people disappear. He has a friend down in Florida somewhere. I think it is the man you have been referring to as Duck. He has an army there and in New York."

"The Mafia?" Chet asked.

"Maybe," she replied nodding. "I'm not sure. You have to understand. I tried to stay hidden while I was at Mr. Archibald's. I heard things, but I don't know what they mean." John nodded. He needed to treat this interview with kid gloves. Rosa might be a gold mine of information, but he didn't want to upset her and not get anything out of her. Chet was grinning. John gave him a confused look.

"She said Duck had an army," Chet said. "One of the things that Duck told me was how much Archibald admired Luciano for control of the Commission. The other thing he admired him for was what he believed was his involvement during World War II. There are many different stories about what happened during World War II with Luciano, but Archibald likes to believe that Luciano raised his own private army. Have you guys noticed his mansion? Armed thugs are everywhere."

"Do you think they're Mafia?" Trip asked. Chet shook his head.

"Trip, say what you want about Archibald," Chet began. "He follows the law of Cosa Nostra. His mother or father is not of direct Italian descent, so he cannot join. The same way neither John nor Mark could join, even though both helped them out. I don't think the men are made men. I have a theory, but I couldn't prove it." Trip raised an eyebrow. John smiled and waved Chet on. "I think he may have created his own Omerta." Chet was very disappointed. He thought everyone would gasp or be in shock, but all he saw was blank looks on almost everyone's face, except for John who was smiling and for Rosa who was nodding. It then dawned on Chet that Rosa nodding meant he was right; Archibald had created his own Omerta.

Chapter 42

"What is an Omerta?" Jessica asked. Chet was ignoring her and was on one knee in front of Rosa. John thought if he didn't know better that Chet was going to propose to her.

"Did he have a ceremony?" Chet asked, quite excited. Rosa shook her head no. Chet's face fell. John was chuckling at Chet. He turned to Jessica and began to explain.

"Omerta is the code of silence or code of honor that the Mafia lives by. While it is taken very seriously, I don't think some of these current wiseguys live up to it like made men did in the past. Many of the men we arrested flipped quickly once we arrested them. The essence of Omerta is like a trip to Vegas. What happens stays within the group, hence the saying 'This Thing of Ours.'" John turned toward Rosa. "Did Archibald stress honor and a code of silence?" Rosa nodded. Chet turned toward John and sighed. John smiled at his friend. "Did you really think she was going to witness the blood oath?"

"I could hope," Chet replied. John laughed loudly. Chet loved conspiracies and secret societies.

"There's a blood oath?" Jessica asked. Chet nodded solemnly. John was beginning to think that Archibald and Chet had a little something in common when it came to fascination with the Mafia. Arthur had been listening to the entire story by Chet, but he seemed a little confused.

"Ok, Chet," Arthur began. "I get Archibald has this love for Lucky Luciano. I mean, I knew that. He has books galore on the man and will go on and on about him if you make the mistake of getting him started. What I don't understand is what this has to do with anything."

John nodded and looked at Chet.

"May I?" John asked Chet. Chet took a chair and offered John the floor.

"I'm going on what I figured out while you were talking, so feel free to jump in if I mess up Chet," John said. Chet nodded. John turned to face the room.

"Let's start at the beginning," John said as he turned toward the timeline. "For the purposes of our discussion, I believe that would be the death of Edward Gates." John watched Jeremiah to make sure he was still with him. Jeremiah nodded, and John continued. "This was the point where I was inserted into the investigation, by your own account, Trip, something you never quite understood." Trip nodded.

"It's nothing against you, John," Trip said. "It just never made sense to put someone as good as a detective as you undercover given how little it used your talents."

"Agreed," John said. Jessica was surprised. "All I was doing was gathering evidence, not digging or using my detective skills. You have to admit it really doesn't make sense. Point number two: it's around this time that Duck goes off the radar, and all evidence that links him to the Mafia disappears." John noticed that Rosa was nowhere to be seen and paused. "Where's Rosa?"

"Making us some burgers," Jessica replied. "Do you need her in here?"

"I can hear everything," she called from the kitchen. John chuckled. "I'll be just a minute, John. Is that ok?"

"Take your time, Rosa, and don't worry about him," Jessica called back. Rosa came through the door with a tray of burgers. She started to serve everyone but John. John looked around, surprised. "Calm down, you big baby," Jessica said to him. "Everyone else wanted cheeseburgers. We know you think that's somewhat un-American." Jessica held a hand up before he could speak. "She also knows you only want mustard, pickle, and onion on it."

"What is it about you and food?" Trip asked. John was watching this like someone watching a tennis match.

"It's part of his thing," Jessica replied. "Sam said that some things are no big deal to him with food, and others are national tragedies if you don't get them the way he wants them. Before you ask, John, I told her how you wanted your burger."

"How do you know?" John asked.

"Everyone does," she replied as the whole room nodded.

"What about you and your cheesecake?" John asked. Jessica pointed a finger at John as she began, and Trip nearly choked on his food from laughter.

"Cheesecake is perfect the way it is," she replied. "Now, get on with the story."

Chapter 43

John shook his head but decided to continue with the story.

"So, we've got Duck out of the way and Anthony Lucciano and his men found guilty of a mess of charges." Jeremiah was staring at John.

"Boy, are you saying that Duck, Archibald, and this third man set up the Mafia to be arrested? Are you saying those three men manipulated the FBI into doing their dirty work?" Jeremiah asked John. John looked at Chet who was smiling.

"You look at what the Commission did, and it has a lot of similarities," Chet said. "But, it's the bigger picture you're missing." Jeremiah, intrigued, signaled for him to continue. "Archibald has his own personal army now in the current Mafia." Chet could tell by the look on Jeremiah's face that he was having trouble buying that explanation.

"Look, all of the current members that are in place are there because of what happened. Duck has no business being the head of the current family in New York, and now, apparently, in Florida." John nodded to that statement. "Everyone has loyalty to Archibald, Duck, and this other person because of what they've done. Think about it. It was a bloodless coup, and Archibald has friends now in power positions." Jeremiah thought for a minute. He was rubbing his chin as Rosa brought John his burgers. John smiled, thanked her, and began to dig in. Jeremiah was slowly pacing while thinking. He walked over to Trip, who was considering the idea John and Chet had presented himself.

"What do you think?" Trip asked Jeremiah.

"It's a stretch," Jeremiah responded. "I mean, someone would have to be the most egotistical, conceited, narcissistic, vile excuse of a human being that ever lived."

100

Jessica thought about what Jeremiah said, leaned in close to John, and whispered in his ear.

"Didn't he basically repeat himself?" she asked quietly. John nodded.

"Jeremiah likes to make sure you know what he thinks of Archibald," John replied, just as quiet. Jessica nodded and leaned back. Jeremiah hadn't noticed the conversation.

"It would take a lot of power, money, and pure evil to pull off something like that," Jeremiah said, tapping his finger on his lip as he thought.

"Sounds just like Archibald to me," Trip said. Jeremiah looked over at Trip, smiling and nodded. Rosa had sat back down. John had noticed she was acting like she had something to say. Rosa saw his glance, and John smiled encouragingly.

"You don't have it quite right," she said softly. Everyone turned toward her. She seemed even more nervous. Madeline squeezed Rosa's hand, and Jessica smiled at her encouragingly. "Archibald doesn't expect loyalty; he demands it. He believes he owns his men, like cattle." John watched her and found the words she used interesting.

"Rosa, would he be above buying or selling them, like cattle?" John asked.

"He did me," Chet said softly.

Chapter 44

"I don't mean to be insensitive, and nothing would make me happier than seeing Archibald get exactly what is coming to him," Arthur began. "But, what has all of this got to do with the murder of our daughter?"

"Isn't it obvious," Madeline replied. "John got too close, and they killed Sam to back him off."

"Why not kill John? No offense, John," Arthur added quickly.

"None taken," he replied.

"Because, dear," Madeline responded. "Killing an FBI agent would bring down the entire FBI on them." John thought about it for a minute. That just didn't work for him. He was sure Sam wasn't killed in a mob hit. He noticed Arthur watching him.

"A few nights ago, I asked you if the mob killed her, and you said no. Now, if they did, I can take it. I just need to know." Arthur was nearly pleading with John.

"I don't think they did, Arthur," John replied, shaking his head. "We're missing something. I'm sure of it."

"I think it's obvious," Jessica replied. "Archibald, Duck, and this other person didn't want the law coming down on them." She turned and looked at Jeremiah. "They didn't want you to be President, and they killed Sam so you'd pull out of the Presidential race."

"That makes a lot of sense," Chet said. Jeremiah thought about it and looked at Trip. Trip nodded slowly. John realized that Trip truly thought this was a possibility, but it was obvious to John that Jeremiah did not.

As John watched the two men, it was like a huge lock clicked in his head. It was so obvious to him not only who the third man of the cabal was, but why. It made perfect sense with everything he had learned today. Whoever killed Sam did so because of the three men, John was sure of it. Jeremiah avoided John's gaze. He looked out over the room.

"I never considered that," he lied. To John, he might as well have been jumping up and down, screaming, "Liar, Liar, pants on fire!" John thought he would be sick. He was pretty sure he knew why Jeremiah was lying. He was also pretty sure he knew who the third member of the cabal was. It was the only thing that made sense. John couldn't believe it was scarcely a few days ago he had looked at the man who had his wife killed, the leader of the free world, President of the United States of America, Kenneth Nichols.

Chapter 45

John excused himself for a second. He told everyone he wasn't feeling well, and headed outside to get some fresh air. Jessica followed after him to see if he was alright. Jeremiah's heart sank.

"That boy knows," he thought to himself. "I shouldn't be surprised; Sam always said he could figure anything out." The Senator was about to follow after them when Trip stopped him.

"Sir," Trip began, hesitating.

"Spit it out, Son. I'm not getting any younger." Jeremiah realized he was a bit rude, but he was more worried about John.

"Sir, I don't completely believe what Jessica said, and furthermore, I don't think you do either," Trip said quietly. Jeremiah had been looking to see where John went outside, but with Trip's revelation, he turned to face him.

"So, I see you finally decided to be the leader you can be," Jeremiah replied just as quietly. Trip jerked with surprise. "Oh come on now, Boy. You know everyone called you By the Book Lionel."

"I really hate that name," Trip said, disgusted.

"You think Jeremiah is my first choice?" the senator asked. Trip chuckled. Jeremiah smiled and then turned serious. "You do know why I agreed with the fair Jessica?" Trip nodded. "Do we agree that we cannot, under any circumstances, tell them?" Trip nodded again. "Then what are we going to do about John?" Trip groaned and half closed his eyes. He sighed and shook his head.

"I swear that man is going to be the death of me," Trip said, looking to see where John had gone.

"That ability of his can be a trifle unsettling," Jeremiah replied. "Let me try to talk to him." Trip nodded, and Jeremiah headed outside to try and find John. Jessica was heading back to the house and smiled when she saw Jeremiah.

"He says he's fine," Jessica said.

"Is he?" Jeremiah asked. Jessica shrugged. "Are you ok? More importantly, are the two of you ok?" Jessica shrugged again and smiled.

"What can I tell you, Jeremiah?" Jessica responded. "Go talk to him. He could use a friend." Jessica headed up the path toward the house. Jeremiah turned and saw John. John was staring at Jeremiah.

"Jessica is right," John said. "What I could use right now is a friend. I could use a friend that won't lie to me." Jeremiah sighed.

Chapter 46

"You think Kenneth Nichols had something to do with Sam's death," John stated flatly.

"I never said that," Jeremiah replied firmly.

"You don't have to," John retorted.

"Boy," Jeremiah said drawing himself up. "You don't know who you're dealing with!"

"I know I'm dealing with a man that you thought you should run against, a man who was the sitting Vice President of the United States. As a member of HIS party, you ran against him in the primaries and only pulled out after Sam died. Jeremiah everyone knew you were going to beat him, EVERYONE!" John was fighting off emotion but not doing a very good job. He continued. "You thought so little of him. It was clear to anyone who watched you debate! You know something, something you're not telling me!"

"I CAN'T TELL YOU!" Jeremiah screamed. The two men stared at each other. One thought of Sam and John as the children he never had, and the other thought of Jeremiah as his second father. The tension was apparent to anyone that walked outside.

"Then, it's obvious we have nothing to discuss if Sam's death means so little to you," John said barely above a whisper. Jeremiah crossed the distance between them quickly. If John didn't know better, he thought Jeremiah was going to strike him. Jeremiah's face was inches from John's.

"I have put up with your all-knowing, holier-than-thou attitude for too long today, Boy! Do you know who I AM!?" John was taken aback; he had never heard Jeremiah talk to anyone that way before.

"You're the man who won't tell me who killed my wife," John hissed. Jeremiah almost raised his fist but stopped himself. John couldn't stop himself, and the verbal assault continued. "I see you really are just like all other

106

politicians, say whatever it takes, but when push comes to shove, you protect yourself rather than do what you say you're going to do."

Jeremiah looked like he had been slapped. Anger flashed all over his face.

"Listen good Boy, because I'll only say this once," Jeremiah said in an intense whisper. "IF, and I'm not saying he did, but IF he did, what makes you think he won't slaughter every one of you on nothing more than a whim?" John was taken by surprise. His mind was whirling. He had misread things earlier. John thought Jeremiah was keeping secrets because of his new political appointment. Jeremiah was keeping things secret because he was scared. Jeremiah Cosby was scared of Kenneth Nichols.

Chapter 47

"You've been so sure of yourself for so long that you do not have a clue how normal people live in everyday life, do you John?" The Senator asked him. "I can say, with my position, I do not know how Mister and Misses Jones live. What I do know is that Mister and Misses Jones do not know what it is like to see people with enormous amounts of power do things that are not only illegal, but highly immoral. These people in power are not scared of the law. They are above the law. Your friend Chet is a lot closer to the truth than you realize. I do believe that Archibald and his friends have formed a modern day Commission and even have their own Murder Inc. John, they are untouchable!" John studied Jeremiah. Every word Jeremiah said, John believed. John sighed.

"Jeremiah, I have nothing to lose," he said quietly.

"Four years ago, that may have been true, Son," Jeremiah said, laying his hand on John's shoulder. "There is a beautiful, young lady in there that would completely disagree with that statement. John, you have everything to lose."

"I owe Sam," John replied, never looking at Jeremiah.

"You do not owe her your life," Jeremiah stated simply.

"That's just it, Jeremiah," John said as he jammed his hands into his pockets. "I do. I ruined hers, and it's up to me to make things right. Don't' you understand? All she wanted to do was be a mom and have kids. Now I find out someone raped her, and she lost her child and thought she lost the ability to ever have one. Then she was pregnant, and I didn't even notice! I —the guy who can see and figure out anything— I missed it! " John was very emotional. His next words were a whisper. "Then, she was killed, so I do owe her my life. I have to do everything I can to put them all away." The silence between them was deafening. Jeremiah broke it, quietly.

"What if you cannot?"

"I'll die trying," John said, looking Jeremiah right in the eye. Jeremiah sighed.

"Boy, you'va got battle craziness," Jeremiah said, shaking his head. "No one is asking you to do this."

"I've got to do it," John replied. Jeremiah nodded.

"John, you cannot pull them into this; it could be career suicide. It could be actual suicide." John looked at his old friend and saw he was telling the truth. John nodded.

"I won't do anything until I have proof," John said. He barked a laugh. "Besides, who would believe me that one of the most beloved Presidents in the United States had something to do with the murder of my wife?" John was watching Jeremiah. When he said beloved, Jeremiah looked like he wanted to spit. John smiled at him, and Jeremiah got a rueful grin on his face. John decided it was time to apologize for his earlier outburst. "Look, about earlier . . ." Jeremiah chuckled.

"We are old friends, John," Jeremiah said, bailing John out of trying to think up an apology. "These things happen, my boy. Just do me a favor. Do not go after them with a suicide wish. They will gladly grant it." Jeremiah clapped John on the shoulder and walked inside. John looked over the garden, half expecting to see Sam. John gathered himself and started back inside, knowing that the conversation he just had must remain private.

Outside the Daily Grind Gentleman's Club
New York, New York

Chapter 48

Ernie looked up and down the street. He was hoping for some good business today with his hotdog cart. He hoped for it every day. He pushed his cart past the old Mafia hangout and thought for what must have been the thousandth time about purchasing it. He glanced at it for a minute. He had dreams of turning it into a burger joint. He had an idea for making a place called Four Fellas. He chuckled every time he thought about it. He figured that other burger joint would sue him, but it had to be more exciting than the life he was currently living. That was the last thought he had as the wall of the former strip club beside him blew apart and landed on top of him, crushing the life out of him.

When the FBI was notified a few hours later, they would come to learn that three separate explosions happened in the state within a minute of each other. At each explosion, there were personal effects of current FBI agent John Fowler found. When the initial investigation began into the death of Pamela Davis, it was found the last paperwork she handled was the release of David George. The paperwork was signed by John Fowler, FBI. As the evidence began quickly pile up against John Fowler, the Director of the FBI was made aware of what was going on. The Director told the lead agent on the case to bring in John Fowler. The Director picked up the folder sent to him by Trip from the New York Office and looked it over again. After a minute, he called the agent back and told him that he was only bringing John in for questioning and to assist on the case.

In New York, Jeff Hart hung up the phone. He turned to his partner, Steve McIntosh. Just a few days ago, they had been dressed down by John at the Archibald estate. Archibald had decided that they had been treated unfairly and helped the two gentlemen by paying off a large portion of their student loan debt. The men owed Archibald, and they thought nothing would make him happier than making John look like a fool. Jeff called two of their FBI buddies that were stationed in Washington, D.C. and told them what was going on with John Fowler. The two men agreed to help after Jeff told them that Archibald might be able to assist them. Jeff hung up with his friends and told Steve the good news. Jeff took out a burner cell phone and made a call to Archibald.

Chapter 49

Archibald was surprised when one of his burner phones was brought to him with his two newest assets in the FBI on the other line. He was even more surprised, but very happy, to hear the mess John was in. Archibald assured Jeff his two friends would be taken care of. Two minutes later, Archibald hung up with Duck. Archibald had paid off their private loans as well. He now had four men in the FBI that were loyal to him. Archibald had studied not only the Mafia, but the Red Mafiya, the Russian equivalent of La Cosa Nostra. The greatest lesson Archibald learned was everyone had a price, especially those who thought they were underappreciated. Archibald called Kenneth to give him the good news.

"You realize this is probably Bruce's doing?" Kenneth asked. Archibald chuckled.

"It does resemble our deranged friend," Archibald replied. "Do we want to try to stop it?" Kenneth laughed heartily.

"No," Kenneth replied through laughter. "Let him dirty his hands while we take care of more important things. Is there anything else I should know?"

"Is it safe to talk business?" Archibald asked.

"Yes, but you'll have to be quick. There's a press conference in a few minutes," the outgoing President replied.

"We have a shipment ready to go; do you want to hold off until all of this blows over?" Archibald asked.

"Is there any evidence that anyone knows what we are doing?" Kenneth asked as his reply.

"None that I am aware of," Archibald answered.

"Then let's go ahead," Kenneth replied. "We wouldn't want to upset our African friends."

"Or any of the others," Archibald replied with a smile on his face. "Take care Kenneth. We'll meet soon."

"I will, my friend," Kenneth replied and disconnected the line. Kenneth got up, knocked on the door, and the secret service answered. Kenneth walked to his last conference, flanked by the armed escort.

"That will be the one thing I don't miss about this job," he thought as they headed down the red carpeted hall.

John Fowler
The Moores'

Chapter 50

Jessica met John at the door as he started back inside.

"We need to talk," she said to him. John had never seen her quite this serious looking before. He waited for her to go on. "Listen, John, you're about to come to blows with people over this thing. Maybe you aren't ready." John listened, but inside, he was ready to explode.

"So let me get this straight," he began. "Everyone wants me to solve the case, but when I do what I do, everyone gets upset. Jessica, listen to me. I am a mess as a person. This isn't something that's because of the drinking, or the death of Sam. It's who I am. I don't relate to people like everyone else does. If you tell me to go do something, then I move heaven and earth to do it. If you want something sniffed out, then I will sniff it out, plus every little dirty secret. Don't you get it!? I don't play well with others. This group of people are my only friends, and look at how I treat them! If you want me to find Sam's killer, then I've got to do it my way."

Jessica listened. She didn't like what she heard, but she knew he was right. This is what Sam had always talked about. John had so much trouble with . . .well, stuff. When Jessica didn't speak, John continued.

"Trip and Jeremiah claim to want to help, but it's obvious they both know things or think things," he said, almost pleading.

"It's not like that," Jessica said, trying to convince herself as much as him. "John, they have so many things they have to juggle."

"I don't," John replied simply. Jessica looked like she had been slapped. "Listen, I'm not going anywhere in the FBI because I rub too many people the wrong way."

"That's not true," Jessica said. "There's been some people that could be considered difficult to work with that have advanced in the FBI."

"They're all in Washington," John replied. "I have no desire to move there, and besides, one is some great psychologist profiler, and the other one was stuck in a basement." Jessica smiled at the last part. "Look, Trip and Jeremiah knew something and didn't tell me. This would be so much easier if it wasn't for this stupid political stuff that I don't have the stomach or the time for. Either they want me to solve the case, or they don't."

"Don't give me that," Jessica said with a twinkle in her eye. "You're as likely to give up this case as you are to miss the national championship game in college basketball."

"Who's playing?" John asked, trying not to grin. Jessica grabbed John by his shirt and pulled him in for a kiss. After a few seconds, he broke the kiss. Jessica was giving him a look that was making his knees melt. "What was that for? Not that I'm complaining," he added quickly.

"For being you," she replied, letting him go and walking back inside.

Chapter 51

John watched Jessica walk off and shook his head. It was days like these he missed Sam. She understood him. She didn't always agree with him, but she understood him. Except for his parents, he really thought Sam was the only person to ever get him. Everything to John was black and white. It was just that simple, except it wasn't to anyone else. He really thought Jessica was trying to understand him but didn't. John worried that Jessica found that part of him mysterious or something like that. John shook his head. He wasn't going to think about women. He had to get his mind on something less complicated, like nuclear fission or the true purpose of Stonehenge.

Trip and Jeremiah walked up to John. This was getting more fun for John by the second. He started to speak when Trip held up his hand.

"Look," Trip began. "We haven't worked with you on a case for a while, and the two of us should have told you our reservations up front and that there were some things we couldn't discuss. We've made today harder on you than necessary. You've heard things today that no one would take well. You did Sam right today, John. You fought for her. When you get in positions like ours, sometimes you get caught up in the games that have nothing to do with the real issues. For you, it's simple. You want to find out who killed Sam, and you don't care who you upset to do it. I don't know about the Senator, but some days, as much trouble as it causes, I wish more people were like you. It would cut through red tape that seems to choke us in our jobs more and more each day." The Senator looked at Trip, and then over to John.

"What he said," the Senator deadpanned. John exploded with laughter. It had been such a trying day for him. He needed the release and laughed until his sides hurt. The three men walked back into the living room together. Rosa was looking very nervous. John knew it was time to talk to her and find out what she knew, if anything. He knew she was worried Archibald might find her, but she had insisted on being here to try to help John find out who killed Sam, and Trip and Rosa's friend Thelma.

"John," she said, approaching him. "I need to talk to you."

"Ok, Rosa," he responded. "Just me, or everyone?" Rosa looked around the room and nodded.

"I think you all need to hear this," she replied.

Chapter 52

Rosa looked around the room and began.

"I think Mr. Archibald is making people disappear," she began. John raised his eyebrows. Rosa continued. "I told you earlier about how I think Duck is doing things down in Florida. Well, I think they are shipping people out of the country."

"Out of the country?" John asked. "Rosa, are you sure? I mean, that's huge. That's something that surely the FBI would be made aware of." Rosa looked a little disappointed. Jeremiah was studying John. He knew John was close to figuring out things he wasn't allowed to tell. He just had to give John a little push

"John, why don't you talk to your friend in the CIA about Duck and Archibald?" Jeremiah asked. "You know, Mitchell Franks?" John turned and looked at Jeremiah with surprise.

"The CIA?" John asked. "Jeremiah, you know that the CIA can't have a file on a United States citizen unless they are suspected of participating in illegal activities on foreign soil." Jessica had been standing behind the couch listening to this exchange. She sighed, walked up to John, and tapped him on the shoulder. He turned to look at her. She gave him a look like he was an idiot. John thought about what he just said. It was like a light bulb came on over John's head.

"OH!!" John exclaimed. "So, there is a file on Archibald because he is suspected of illegal activity on foreign soil!" Jessica patted him on the shoulder like you would a toddler for getting something right, while Trip just smacked his own hand against his forehead. Jessica shook her head and looked at Rosa.

"Human trafficking?" Jessica asked. Rosa shrugged, confused. "Do you understand what I'm asking?" Jessica asked. Rosa shook her head no. "Are they kidnapping people and selling them for things like sex slaves or some other ungodly thing?" Rosa thought for a second. She looked at John and back at Jessica. John shot Jessica a look to back off before she began to full-on grill Rosa. He needed to really handle this with kid-gloves.

"Rosa," John began encouragingly. "What do you think is happening?"

"Well, you know how Mr. Archibald thinks that I'm an illegal alien and can't speak English?" She looked around the room to make sure everyone was with her. When she was satisfied they were, she continued. "He said something once to Duck about making me disappear with the rest of them. I don't know who the rest of them are, but I think that Archibald's men are taking illegal aliens, or those that they think are illegal, and selling them to people in other countries. They are selling them everywhere from what I can tell. I know there is some place in South America or South Africa, or somewhere that they sell them. They use them to mine something." She was trying to think. "They call them red stones, or red rocks." Chet and John exchanged a look. John knew he should know what she was talking about. He looked around the room and caught the sunlight streaming in the room glinting off Madeline's engagement ring. He sucked in breath as it hit him.

"Blood diamonds," John said softly to Chet. Chet's eyes widened, and he let out a whistle as he looked at John. They both looked at Rosa. "Did they say Blood Diamonds?" John asked. Rosa nodded. Madeline looked very confused. John nodded to Chet. Chet began to explain.

"Simply put, Blood Diamonds, or conflict diamonds, are regular diamonds that are mined in a war zone and are sold to pay for weapons or other things to fight the wars with." Chet looked around to make sure everyone was on the same page and saw that they were.

119

"But, that's not all the only place they send the people they have kidnapped," Rosa continued. "He sends them anywhere that people will pay for them." Jessica looked confused.

"This doesn't make any sense," she said.

"Actually, it's brilliant," Trip replied. Jessica looked at him, shocked. Trip shrugged. "It's heinous and evil, but absolutely brilliant. Think about it. Illegal aliens are kidnapped. Who's going to report it?" Trip looked around the room, letting it sink in. Jessica looked horrified.

"But, it's slavery!" Jessica exclaimed.

"And, Archibald's daughter killed someone because of how her association with Beth might affect Veronica's standing in life," the Senator said quietly.

"She was gay!" Jessica shouted. "Veronica killed Beth because Veronica was afraid someone might think she was gay for being associated with Beth!"

"No, my dear. Veronica killed Beth simply because she didn't conform to what Veronica thought she should be," Jeremiah responded gently. "Now, it was the fact that she was not heterosexual that caused that lack of conformity in Veronica's mind. I dare say that if Veronica had learned Beth was of some mixed race that included an ethnic minority, she would have killed her as well," Jeremiah paused. "Where do you think she learned this sickness from, dear?" Jessica looked sick to her stomach.

"How do they get away with it?" John asked, concentrating on the problem and trying to steer the conversation back on track. He knew that would upset Jessica, but he felt they were so close that he would chance Jessica's wrath. Rosa nodded and turned toward Chet.

"You were right about Mr. Archibald, Chet," Rosa said to Chet. "But, he also studies all criminal masterminds. He simply pays off someone who has been done wrong, looked over, or even just not been properly thanked the way someone thinks they should be." John repeated that sentence over and over in his head. Alarm bells were going off inside. Three FBI officers jumped into his head, and when he turned and looked at the father of one of them, John saw the Senator had the same thought.

Chapter 53

"Chet, get your laptop," John said with a sense of urgency in his voice. Chet had heard that tone before and didn't question anything. He ran into the other room to get it. Trip knew that tone as well. He walked over to John.

"What's going on? What did I miss?" Trip asked. John turned to Jessica.

"When you and I grabbed Rosa and got her out of there, we put Jeff and Steve in charge, right?" John asked Jessica. Jessica nodded. "Was there any chance Archibald saw me speak to those two?" Jessica thought and nodded, smiling. John's face fell. Chet ran back into the room.

"Run financials on Jeff Hart and Steve McIntosh," John told Chet.

"Don't you think you should ask me first?" Trip asked. "I am in charge."

John turned to face Trip.

"Trip," John began. "I have every reason to believe that Archibald saw me chew out those two agents, and after what Rosa just said—," It immediately dawned on Trip what John was implying. Trip interrupted John.

"You heard him, Chet! Run those financials!" Chet began running his program. While that was going on, Arthur, who was bored, turned on the TV. The news was covering multiple explosions in, and around, New York City. John glanced at the TV, turned toward Chet, and then whipped his head back around at the TV, after realizing what he was seeing. Trip saw the area on TV and turned toward John.

"Why do I know this place?" Trip asked.

"It's the strip club I was talking about earlier, The Daily Grind," John answered softly. Jessica and Trip exchanged glances and turned to face the TV and John. About that time, the TV switched from the gentleman's club to the psychiatric hospital outside of the city. A picture of David George flashed up. Underneath his picture

122

was one word: Escaped? John's mind was connecting dots quickly. The TV changed to the remains of Pamela Davis's home. John knew immediately what had happened. He turned from the TV toward Chet. Jessica and Trip kept their eyes on John. John ignored them and was watching Chet work. Chet stopped, turned toward John, and smiled.

"Right again, John," Chet said. "Their private student loans have been forgiven." Chet turned toward Rosa. "Is this the way he normally does things?"

"Sometimes," she replied. "Sometimes, he buys small banks or helps out loan officers with their personal loans if he knows one of his marks is going to try to pay off the loan. Once the mark takes out the new loan to pay off the one he or she owes Archibald, they find they're right back in Archibald's pocket again. He likes to brag about how that rips out their heart, or breaks their spirit or will." Trip rubbed his hand over his head.

"It's ingenious," he said, impressed. John was writing something down on a piece of paper. He folded it and handed it to Chet.

"I need you all to trust me," John said to everyone. "Chet and only Chet will read this paper. If I'm right, you'll all know what I wrote in less than an hour." Trip sighed and nodded reluctantly.

Chapter 54

Jeremiah was watching the TV and all of the carnage that was being covered.

"What kind of animal would do this?" he asked no one in particular, quietly. John didn't necessarily think it was Bruce, but he could see by the looks on Chet's, Trip's, and Jessica's faces that they did. John walked over and laid a hand on Jeremiah's shoulder. Jeremiah glanced at John, then at the TV, then back at John, confused. Jeremiah looked over at Jessica and saw the sad look on her face. As it started to dawn on the Senator, he looked over at Trip for confirmation. Trip was running his hand over his head, looking very uncomfortable.

"Oh," Jeremiah said quietly, his shoulders slumping. Jessica crossed the room and hugged the Senator.

"It's not your fault," Jessica said. "You didn't raise him like this."

"It's like a piece of his soul is corrupted or doesn't even exist," Jeremiah said softly. John looked over at Trip at that comment. Trip was nodding as he thought about it.

"Senator," Trip asked quietly. "Did you know Bruce's psych evaluation is missing from his personnel file?" Jeremiah had disengaged himself from Jessica's hug and turned toward Trip with anger on his face.

"So, I'm not crazy!" Jeremiah exclaimed. John and Trip both looked confused. "I never understood how that boy got past all of the FBI tests!" John felt the lock turn in his head. There was only one person he could think of that could pull something like that off. John looked over at the timeline Chet had laid out. Kenneth Nichols, the youngest Vice President in the history of the United States, had been elected to that position just a few months before Bruce had joined the FBI. It was all making sense to John. John saw Jeremiah looking at him. Jeremiah barely nodded at him. That was all the confirmation John needed. He was sure

124

Jeremiah didn't know for sure, but he had suspected that Bruce got into the FBI because of Kenneth Nichols. That made Bruce the inside man for the cabal. Everything was slowly falling into place.

John slowly turned to look at the TV screen. He thought he had very little time left in this group meeting. There were so many things he wanted to ask Rosa, but he knew he had to pick one thing that could nail the entire cabal, if it did exist.

"Rosa," John began. "Is there any chance that you saw either Duck or this other mysterious person at Archibald's home?" Rosa shook her head no. John knew that had been a long shot. There was too much to still unravel.

"But, I did hear him talk to a FBI agent about the Senator," she added. John smiled at her.

"Thanks, Rosa, but Archibald already turned over the tape of his and Luke's meeting," John said. "I'm afraid Archibald would say he was only trying to help Bruce find his dad. If Bruce is the killer we're looking for, I don't think any of us would be shocked to hear he had something to do with his father's disappearance." John looked over at Jeremiah, who was nodding. Jeremiah looked like his heart was being ripped out. John couldn't imagine the pain of your own child trying to destroy you.

"I don't think you understand," Rosa said. "Twice, I heard him tell how he stopped the Senator from getting elected President and it had to do both times with the FBI agent that I think killed Thelma."

Chapter 55

John turned first to make sure Trip was ok. He looked ready to explode, but Trip managed to stay in control. Trip nodded for John to continue. John turned back to Rosa.

"Exactly what are you talking about?" John asked Rosa, trying to stay calm.

"It was during the primary when the Senator was running for President. I first heard him tell the man he respects so much that he would make sure the Senator didn't run," Rosa replied. John nearly did a dance. He urged her to continue. "Archibald said he could tell their crazy friend something that would take care of everything. He didn't say anything for a minute, and then, he told the man on the phone that his plan was better. He told the man on the other end that he would give him the final push if he would drop the bomb. I think that's what he said, drop the bomb." Rosa looked around, worried she had said something wrong. Jeremiah looked sick. Madeline and Arthur were telling him it wasn't his fault. John knew exactly what had happened. He knew he would have a hard time getting the proof he needed, but he was certain what had happened. Chet and Jessica were exchanging nervous looks.

"Do you have any idea who the other man was? Was it Duck?" Jessica asked Rosa. She shook her head no. John was taking stock of the room. From what he could tell, Jeremiah knew. He didn't think Madeline or Arthur knew it was Kenneth, but they did know something. He was positive Chet and Jessica didn't know, but he couldn't quite tell with Trip.

"You said there was two times?" John asked Rosa, gently.

"The other time he was telling the story to his daughter, but Archibald made it seem like it was something that just came up and he took advantage of. It wasn't like he planned it. I know he did though! He and that man on the phone planned it." She turned toward Jessica. "I'm sure it wasn't Duck. He doesn't talk to Duck like that. Duck doesn't talk on the phone long." Rosa paused and looked at Trip, and continued.

"That was also when he told his daughter that Bruce had to take care of a loose end. They were talking about Thelma. Veronica had stormed in earlier with the paper that had the story of her death in it. Veronica asked him about it, and that's when he told her about Bruce. I'm sorry. You know she cared for you, right?" Trip nodded, with tears in his eyes.

John walked over and sat down beside Jessica on the couch. He fought the urge to tell her what he believed had happened. He was going to need a lot of proof to bring down the man responsible for all of this. John needed more and didn't think he had much time.

"Rosa," John began. "What's his biggest weakness?" Rosa looked at John, confused. "What upsets him or gets him off his game?" Rosa thought for a minute.

"Well," she began. "Archibald doesn't like anyone to question his authority. He wants everyone to know he is the one in charge. I once heard some of his men talking. They would say things like he wants everyone to know he is the biggest dog in the yard. Does that make sense?" John smiled and nodded. That made perfect sense. Not only did Archibald want to be the one in charge, he wanted everyone to know it. He didn't want anyone to question him.

There was a knock on the door. Rosa went to answer it. Arthur and Madeline did the normal, did you know someone was coming thing. John knew who was at the door. In fact, he was surprised it had taken this long.

Two men pushed passed Rosa and entered the room.

"FBI!" One of the men shouted. "John Fowler, we are here to place you under federal custody. We have reason to believe you have committed acts of terrorism against the United States, specifically the bombing of three different sites in and around the New York City area!" John glanced sideway at Chet. Chet nodded. John stood up, turned away from the agents, and locked his hands behind his head. He was prepared to be handcuffed and led away.

Chapter 56

"Sit down, John," Trip barked. John did as he was told. John looked over at Jessica who smiled at him, despite the situation. They both glanced at Trip who looked like he had had enough of the bad cop, badder cop routine. After what Trip had just learned from Rosa, he was ready to take out his frustration on someone.

"Son, do you know who I am?" Trip asked. One agent looked at the other and shrugged. Trip drew up. "I am Director Lionel Pennyworth Smothers III, the Director of the New York office of the FBI, which means I seriously outrank you. My guess is you aren't the person who made the call to have Agent Fowler detained. So my question to you is does the person who made the call outrank me? And, if he doesn't, are you ready to survive the radioactive fallout of you going over my head when I can tell you agent Fowler has literally been with me, Agent Hammerstein, and Agent Morris for the past four days?"

John was impressed. He didn't think either agent had wet themselves, and he could barely make out that the agent on the left was on the verge of knocking his knees together. John relaxed; it was obvious to him that this was over as quickly as it had started. There might be a little pomp and circumstance from the agents to save face, but when Trip pulled out the 'Lionel Pennyworth Smothers III' card, the game was usually over. Jessica leaned over.

"Was the name enough, or did it take him throwing in the outranking part?" she asked quietly. John tightened the muscles on the left side of his jaw, thinking.

"The one on the left folded at the name," he replied just as quietly, never turning to look at her. "The other held out until the 'radioactive fallout' comment. I must admit, these guys took it better than I thought."

"Any idea what they're talking about, you know, you being brought into custody?" she whispered. John lightly shook his head. He hated to lie to Jessica, but it was necessary to make sure he was right.

"No, but I have a feeling we're done in Virginia for the day," he replied. "We should probably go pack up." Jessica nodded. John was a little upset that Rosa didn't get to tell more of her story, but John had a feeling that what was going on was more important to someone with a much higher rank than John. Jessica nodded, and they both began to get up. Trip turned to look at them.

"Look, we both know that we're going to have to go somewhere with these guys," John began. "I'm guessing New York, but maybe to Quantico. Jessica, Chet and I can go pack. I'm guessing you've never unpacked since you do that suitcase living thing so well." Trip made a weary face at John, but nodded. The three agents left and began to pack.

Jessica and John returned first with suitcases in tow. It was a few minutes later before Chet returned. When he did, he made eye contact with John and nodded just where John could see. Trip was nowhere to be seen while Chet was gone. He returned shortly after Chet. It was obvious some negotiating had been taking place. Trip was on a cell phone. When he saw John, Trip wrapped up the call.

"You're going to be in custody until we can straighten a few things out. We're flying in a helicopter back to New York," Trip said to John with a look of complete seriousness on his face. John really didn't know why every time he saw Trip so serious he wanted to do something to agitate him. John's mind told him not to say what was on the tip of his tongue, but he couldn't resist.

"Will you need to handcuff me? Because if I'm allowed to be near only you, I can't promise I won't try and rub your head," John said with a straight face. Trip stared at John for a second. He then turned to Jessica.

"I'm actually putting him in your custody," Trip said as if John wasn't even there. "If he gets out of line, you have my permission to tase' him, kick him in the groin, punch him in the face, or put him in the submission hold of your choice until he cries like a little baby." Jessica smiled. John looked at her and shuddered. He then turned to the two agents.

"You guys sure you don't want to put me in chains and take me with you?" The two agents shook their heads, turned, and walked to their car. Jessica reached behind John, grabbed his shirt collar, and began to lead him to her vehicle.

"Come on, fugitive," she said.

"You're really enjoying this, aren't you?" John asked.

"Shut up, or I'll get the stun gun out," she replied.

"Yes, ma'am!"

Chapter 57

John was quiet on the way to the helipad and tried to be on the helicopter ride to New York. The two agents that had accompanied them to the helicopter did not join them on the flight. Jessica, John, and Chet sat in the back seat, and Trip sat up front beside the pilot. Trip was constantly working on his phone during the flight. Chet was watching, trying to figure out what was going on, and Jessica was watching Chet trying to see if he was noticing anything. John didn't need his special abilities to know his friends were nervous. He decided to break the silence.

"Have you ever tried stud?" John asked Chet. Chet took a second to analyze the question and then turned toward him. Jessica leaned forward a little and looked at John. He continued. "You know, seven card stud?" Chet nodded.

"I know the game. Why do you ask?" Chet replied. John shrugged.

"It's more math than hold 'em," John replied. "Plus, it's not usually played no-limit, so there's some protection."

"You're talking to a guy with a gambling problem about poker?" Jessica asked incredulously.

"Is that bad?" John asked. Chet snorted.

"It's fine," Chet replied. "I'd just rather talk about something else."

"Ok," John replied. "Do you think I'm about to go to jail? Wait, never mind, you both do." Chet and Jessica's heads snapped around to look at John like he was crazy. John looked from one to the other with a very level gaze. Jessica rolled her eyes and turned to look out the window. Chet stared down at the floor.

"You know, this is probably all good news," John said. Jessica resisted the urge to throw her hands in the air. She didn't resist the eye roll and blowing air up her face from her bottom lip. John smiled. "I'm really touched you two are so worried about me, but if someone thinks I've done something wrong in the FBI and you two have been with me during the time in question, doesn't it beg to ask that this might be a set-up and someone is going to great lengths to frame me?" Chet let a slow grin come across his face. Jessica thought about the statement and played it back in her head. He was right again, and for some reason, that irritated her today. John sat between them, looking smug.

"You're not going to jail, John, I've already taken care of everything," Trip said into his headset. John's smug look fell. "Chet gave me the note before he was supposed to." Jessica turned toward John. She was giving him a very evil look. John actually leaned into Chet trying to lean away from her. Trip ignored them and continued.

"You were right; the two agents that came to arrest you were in Archibald's pocket, but just recently. It appears that Archibald gave the two men the same deal he gave Jeff and Steve. Jeff and Steve think they are in charge of a crime scene in New York. The Director has given us full authority to take over the case. I said what I said back at the Moores' to keep those two agents in the dark. They have already been detained. The Director has put your team in charge."

John felt relief surge through his body. One of his biggest fears was that the Director was one of the people owned by Archibald. Trip continued.

"We've got three separate crime scenes to go through. We're going to start at what's left of The Daily Grind. Jessica, would you like to interrogate Jeff or Steve?" Jessica smiled. John shuddered involuntarily. All he could think about was the old lady John had once seen her interrogate and the session he sat through when Sam died. He felt a moment of sadness for Jeff and Steve. Then, John thought about who the two men had been working for, and the moment quickly passed.

Chapter 58

John, Trip, Chet, and Jessica landed in New York City. A car was waiting for them, and they were whisked to the location of the Daily Grind Gentlemen's club, well, what was left of it. Jessica was driving with Trip in the passenger seat. John and Chet were in the back.

"I can't believe you told them," John began. "I told you not to tell them anything."

"You two argue like an old married couple," Jessica said.

"If he would listen to me, we wouldn't argue," John responded.

"If you wouldn't put me in impossible situations, we wouldn't have these problems," Chet countered.

"As your marriage counselor, knock it off," Trip said, getting irritated. "John, he had to tell me, so I wouldn't be blindsided by those two. Now, when we get to the scene, we're going to take them into custody. I'll take the two numbskulls back to the office and hold them until you three get through looking over the three crime scenes."

"What's the third scene, Trip?" John asked. Trip exchanged a quick glance with Jessica. John had a feeling this wasn't going to be good.

"It's Edward Gates's old home," Trip responded quietly. John set his jaw and nodded. That really didn't surprise him. Trip continued. "There was a body found there. We're double checking fingerprints and confirming with the NYPD." John didn't like where this was going.

"Ricardo?" he asked softly. Trip barely nodded. John turned and looked out the window. "How many?" he asked. Trip looked confused. John didn't see him because he was staring out the window. John turned back to see Trip's confused look. "How many from the undercover days have been found murdered today?"

"We're not sure," Trip responded. "Did you have any contact with Pamela Davis?" John shook his head.

134

"I don't recognize the name," John replied. Trip nodded and glanced back down at his files.

"What about Julie Watson?" Trip asked. "She had a stage name and a hooking name of Tiffany." John closed his eyes. When he opened them, back up he spoke softly.

"I told her she was too smart to be in that life and tried to get her to leave," John replied. "That was another reason they used to call me Saint. They thought I was trying to save everyone." Trip nodded.

"Her body was found at the first crime scene you are going to," Trip said, looking back at the file. "Apparently, there was collateral damage when the building blew, and a hotdog vendor named Ernie was killed in either the blast itself, or the rubble that fell on him." John looked out the window for a second and then back at Trip.

"Someone is trying to get my attention," John said, anger building in his voice. "Whoever it is, they've gotten it. You know the old saying: be careful what you wish for because you might just get it? I'm going to bring this creep down and end this mess." John went back to looking out the window. Jessica and Trip exchanged glances, but neither said anything. For the rest of the ride, everyone rode in silence.

Chapter 59

John got out of the car and began to survey the remains of the building. Chet, Trip, and Jessica got out of the car and headed over to Jeff and Steve. John held back; why he wasn't sure. He had seen something during his initial glance of the scene. He looked around again, and there it was. There was a local cop on the scene. The cop kept glancing at the wall that had been blown apart that used to be the Daily Grind and then to the New York Skyline. He was looking in the direction of where the two towers used to stand.

John had come to New York after 2001. He had never seen the two towers that used to be framed against the sky. Sam used to always talk about how New Yorkers didn't get a fair rap. John used to find them rude. He had grown up in Kentucky, and as far as he was concerned, everyone should have had Southern hospitality. Sam argued with him that New Yorkers dealt with a much faster pace of life. She told him if there was any question of their hospitality, look at how they reacted after the terrible tragedy. John couldn't argue that point with her. He looked at the police officer and decided to approach him. John walked toward him and showed him his badge. The officer nodded and let him have a closer look at the remains of the building and what they could see of the body underneath.

"Everything okay, officer?" John asked. The officer looked at John and shook his head.

"No," he snapped. "This poor guy, all he does is go up and down the street selling his hotdogs. He didn't do nothin' to nobody, and this is what he gets?!" John studied the police officer and looked toward the skyline. He turned and saw the policeman shaking his head at the remains of the wall. John spoke very softly.

"Did you know someone?" John trailed off his thought and nodded toward the skyline. The policeman looked John over, sighed, and began to speak, his demeanor changed.

"My brother," he said simply. "He was a first responder. He was part of the FDNY. Mom wanted him to do something less dangerous than be a cop." The policeman looked away for a minute, then back at John. "It's bad enough some of these clowns killing people, but to use explosives and blow up a building? Hasn't this city seen enough of this?"

John didn't know what to say. Sam would say this was one of those times he just wasn't wired to handle things. He was quiet for a minute as he squatted down to examine the body, and the officer began to talk again.

"I guess you see all sorts of monsters in your line of work?" the officer asked quietly.

"Some, but I never saw one that took as many lives that were taken that day." John stood up and faced the officer. "You're brother, that's the kind of man we need to all strive to be in life. I know you don't know me, but I'd like to thank you for the sacrifice he made."

Tears were in the officer's eyes. He nodded toward John and stuck out his hand. John shook it. The officer walked away quietly to collect himself. John looked over the scene and then back to where the towers should be.

"Lest we never forget," John said softly.

Chapter 60

John walked over to Chet and Jessica who were in the process of detaining Jeff and Steve. When the two men saw John, hatred shot across both of their faces. John knew he should leave things alone, but that wasn't quite his style.

"What's the matter, boys?" John asked, smirking. "You two having to pay for your stupidity?"

"We've already been paid," Steve spat. Jeff groaned.

"Shut up, you idiot!" Jeff yelled at Steve. John glanced over at Jessica. She was truly enjoying this. John leaned in close.

"I told you two that you should have been glad I wasn't the one you reported to the last time you screwed up," John said in a low voice. "Well, I hope you two are ready because I'm going to let Agent Hammerstein over there interrogate you while Chet and I eat popcorn, drink orange soda, and watch on the monitor. Do me a favor. Please don't soil yourself. She really hates that." John leaned away from the two men. Both of them looked a little pale. Trip began to walk them away. Jessica smiled as they heard the two men plead with Trip.

"Listen, I'll tell you everything. I want to make a deal and flip on Archibald," Steve pleaded.

"Forget that! I'll make a deal; just don't put her in there with me!" Jeff exclaimed. As they were taken away, Jessica leaned in where only John could hear her.

"I'm not really that tough in there, am I?" she asked. John tried to swallow quietly where she couldn't hear him. Jessica was good at her job. No, she was great at it, and she enjoyed it, maybe too much. The two biggest stories that ran through the halls of the New York FBI were Jessica's interrogation of John and Jessica's interrogation of an old lady. Now, most stories are exaggerations, but John had witnessed both. One was from behind the glass, and the other he had participated in, unwillingly. John didn't believe any of the stories were exaggerated. In fact, they might have not been truthful enough, from his point of view. Regardless, he was in a spot. He knew he had to answer this question very carefully.

"Yes," he replied simply. "Yes, you are." Jessica looked taken aback. John was reconsidering how he had answered, but it was too late. So he plodded ahead. "Jessica, you are relentless in the box; you took me to pieces."

"I really hated that day," Jessica replied quietly. John gently put his hands on her shoulders and looked her in her eyes.

"You shouldn't apologize for being good at your job," he insisted. "You are the big bomb we can threaten people with. We don't have to detonate the bomb to use it; we can just threaten people with it." John was smiling, thinking he was making her feel better.

"Please don't ever try to cheer me up again," Jessica said with a look of horror on her face.

"It sounded good in my head," John replied honestly. Jessica shook her head, still with the look of horror. John let go of her shoulders. Jessica started to laugh in spite of herself.

"Good grief, John," she said, unable to stop herself from laughing. "That was the most depressing pep talk I have ever heard in my entire life!"

"It really sounded good in my head," John insisted.

"You compared me to a bomb!" She exclaimed.

"People are always saying someone is the bomb," John said defensively.

"You really have no clue," she replied, shaking her head in disbelief. "Come on, Rico Suave, let's go look at the crime scene before you try and cheer anyone else up today."

They headed toward what was left of the doorway of the strip club. The fire chief gave them the ok, and they made their way inside.

Chapter 61

John made his way through the rubble to the interior of the club. Chet looked around the remains.

"What was this place, John?" Chet asked.

"It was a strip club," John replied. "If the girl is who I think she is, she was a student working on a medical degree. She said she couldn't afford tuition to college. Right before we brought down the Mafia, one of her professors found out and exposed her."

"How did he find out?" Jessica asked. John pressed his lips together and blew out his cheeks, not really wanting to answer. It took Jessica about three seconds to figure it out.

"You mean that pervert got to watch, didn't get in trouble, and got her expelled!?!" she screamed. Jessica was furious. She started off through the rubble, muttering to herself about sexist pigs. Chet leaned over to John.

"What did Sam do when she found out?" he asked. John simply nodded his head toward Jessica. Chet chuckled. "You do seem to have a type." John turned toward Chet, puzzled. "You seem to like the ones who won't take your ability as an excuse and push you." Chet thought about what he said. "I don't mean that as a negative. I think you want someone who pushes you to be your best."

John thought about it for a minute. Chet was right. Sam's goal seemed to be to make him the absolute best he could be, no matter how much he complained or tried to stop her. He might have thought about it longer, but Jessica yelled at the two to follow her. They both did without a word. They entered a part of the club John had never been in before. He looked around, trying to get a feel for the room. Jessica noticed.

"You act like you've never been in here before," Jessica said. John simply shook his head no and kept looking the room over. She stepped up to him where she could look him right in the eye. "You're telling me you've never been back here?"

"No, Jessica," he responded. "I've never been in this part of the club. I normally stayed in the back when I was made to come here. I told the boss I didn't feel comfortable out on the floor."

Jessica smiled and shook her head. She started to walk away. John was confused.

"What?" he asked.

"You really are a saint," she responded. The medical examiner had been examining the body that had recently had the rubble from the explosion cleared off it. She bent down beside her. "Is the victim's neck broken?" Jessica asked.

"Yes," the examiner replied. "And, I am pretty sure it was done before this place came tumbling down on top of her. What I don't understand is why put the bomb so far away from the body." Jessica looked at her, confused. "According to the firemen, the way this bomb was set, it was made where it would do the least amount of damage to the victim."

"Do you have a positive ID?" John asked, looking slightly upset.

"We just ran her; she has a couple of priors for solicitation. Her name is Julie Watson," the medical examiner confirmed. John took one last look and walked out of the club. Jessica didn't like the way he looked and chased after him. She caught up with him outside. She came up to him, and John turned to face her.

"After that professor got her expelled, and the Mafia went down, this place closed up," John began. "Julie started working as a prostitute. I felt it was my fault, so I came down here a couple of times to offer her a job, but I chickened out. I would watch her, but I just thought it would be too creepy."

142

Jessica was staring at him in shock. "Well, that explains some things," she said slowly. John raised an eyebrow. "I don't get how watching a hooker from your car isn't creepy, but offering her a job is." John gave her a withering look. Jessica continued. "You know, I told you I followed you a couple of times." John couldn't believe it. She had followed him here! Jessica continued. "I thought you were coming down here to, well you know . . . and well, you chickened out, because of Sam."

"You thought I was going to pay a hooker!" John exclaimed.

"Well, John, she had been dead for a while. I hadn't noticed any women around, so I just thought," Jessica stopped, realizing she was digging the hole even deeper. "I didn't really know you then like I do now. Look, you're a man." As soon as she said it, she wished she hadn't.

"And, men are sexist pigs?" John asked, amazed. Jessica was rubbing her hand against her brow. She really had no good way of answering his question.

"Let's just say I didn't know the whole story and jumped to improper conclusions," she offered.

"Let's," John responded. He walked to the car, wondering when he had entered this twilight zone. Chet was already in the car, sitting in the back. John pointed at him to take the front seat, and Chet shook his head no, refusing. Jessica got in and waited for John to decide what he was going to do. John got in the passenger seat, and the three rode to Edward Gates's former residence.

Chapter 62

After a few moments of uncomfortable silence, Chet decided to try and talk about the case.

"Was there ever any connection to Ricardo Antony and Edward Gates, Boss?" Chet asked.

"Not that I know of, Chet," John replied. "Of course, we still don't know Ricardo's real ID, and given what we're dealing with, we don't want to know his real name to keep his family safe." Jessica had an amused look on her face. John noticed it. "Something funny?"

"Oh, no," Jessica replied. "I just find it interesting that with you gone for almost four years, he still calls you Boss." John smiled, and Chet chuckled. Jessica realized she was missing an inside joke. "Ok, you two, what did I miss?"

"Well," Chet began. "In the beginning, we did it to upset Trip. You know that was our favorite pastime." Jessica rolled her eyes. Early on, John and Chet went out of their way to upset Trip any time they could. Trip wasn't very secure in his original assignment to the New York division of the FBI. And, with Bruce being placed there without Trip being consulted, and the teaming of John, Jessica, and Chet without Trip's permission, Trip became a bit of a control freak.

"One time, he asked me about it," Chet continued. "And I didn't want to tell him we only did it so that we could make him upset, so I gave the answer I called John that because of his love for 80s music." John snickered, and Chet continued. "We've done it for so long just to upset Trip that it's just become second nature to us."

"How come I never knew?" Jessica asked, smiling. John straightened up in the seat and became very interested in the seatbelt. Chet pretended he was getting important information on his cell phone. Jessica kept waiting, and the smile slowly fell from her face. "You two didn't trust me, did you?" she asked accusingly.

144

"Well, Jess," John began. "I mean, you did almost give that lady a heart attack, and if you didn't approve, we were worried what you might do. We didn't want to make you angry, and it wasn't like we were going to stop." Jessica looked as though steam could come off the top of her head.

"How many times do I have to apologize for that!?" John gulped, and Chet tried to hide in the back. Perhaps Jessica wasn't as ready for the truth as John thought. She continued her tirade. "You two and your boys' club!" John cut her off; he didn't feel like rehashing this again.

"For the 300th time, Jessica," John began. "It wasn't a boys' club, or sexism, or anything like that. We protected you like you were our sister. Chet and I constantly came to your defense, but we did treat you like you were our sister, our meddling sister who constantly tattled." Jessica smacked the steering wheel. Chet was in the back seat, laughing at both of them. They both glanced back, not wanting to stop the argument but wondering what was so funny.

"We're back," he said, still laughing. "The band is back together."

"Oh," Jessica began. "That is the most overused saying in all of overused sayings."

"And, here you go again making grand sweeping statements," John countered.

"Oh, yeah?" Jessica replied.

"Yeah," John replied.

"Get a room," Chet chimed in.

"SHUT UP!" John and Jessica said in unison. Chet burst out laughing. John and Jessica tried to fight it off for a few seconds but joined in. After a few minutes, the laughter died down. Chet began to talk.

"Maybe we did go all boys' club on you, Jessica," Chet began. "But, you have to admit when you first started, you were so driven to prove that you belonged.

145

You were a bit of a stick in the mud." John nodded. Jessica backhanded him in the chest with her right hand, but she was smiling as she did.

"Yeah," she begrudgingly admitted. "But, you two could be jerks."

"Could be implies we have stopped," John deadpanned. Jessica gave him a tight smile as they continued down the road toward their destination.

Chapter 63

Jessica pulled up to the home of former witness, Edward Gates. John knew someone was leaving him a message. He was beginning to wonder if his friends weren't right about Bruce being behind this. This was either someone who knew every step of his past by being there or had access to files that told the story of his past.

The main structure of the home was blown apart, but the basement seemed to be relatively intact. The Fire Marshal waved them in, and the three headed downstairs. Another medical examiner was there, studying the corpse. There was little sign of a bomb exploding around the corpse. John got a look at it and thought he might hurl right there.

"Not a pretty sight, eh?" the medical examiner asked. John shook his head and stepped back. "This poor man appears to have been tortured for many days before he was killed. I'll have to get him back to my lab to make sure, of course. Oh, I found this." She pulled out a note that read, "where the rat was found." "I found this in his pocket." John looked at the note and began to think. Chet began thinking out loud.

"Well, I guess Mark was a rat, and he did work at that bar. So, I guess that's what it means," Chet surmised. John frowned. That didn't make sense. What made even less sense was who would have done this. Who would have conducted this hit that was in the Mafia? They were all in jail or in protective custody as far as John knew.

"Chet, have someone run all the men that were involved in the Mafia bust, and make sure no one is out that we don't know about," John said. Jessica walked up to John as Chet made a phone call.

"You think this is mob related?" she asked. John shook his head.

"No," he replied. "But I want to make sure we cover all leads just in case I'm wrong. I do think someone

147

wants us to think that. As far as we know, Ricardo had nothing to do with the Mafia."

"I can check on that," Jessica replied. John nodded, and she walked away to make a phone call. John squatted down and looked over what was left of Ricardo. The medical examiner was watching him.

"Did you know him?" she asked. John nodded. He was sure Ricardo was dead because of something John had done.

"Was his neck broken?" John asked. The medical examiner nodded. John smiled. "But, you can't tell if that killed him until you get him back in the lab." The medical examiner smiled back and nodded.

"You've done this before?" she asked, messing with him.

"Too many times," he replied as he stood up and headed up the stairs.

"Haven't we all?" she replied.

Chapter 64

John stood outside of what was left of the house, emotions rolling though him. John had been positive that Ricardo had been the reason Sam was dead before the meeting of the minds at the Moores'. After he learned what Trip had done, he realized Ricardo probably saved his life. Now, Ricardo was dead, and it was simply because he knew John. John had no question about that. Jessica and Chet approached him. Jessica shook her head when John asked if any of the Mafia members were loose. John wasn't surprised. He knew they still had one more crime scene to look at before they even began to deal with Steve and Jeff back at headquarters.

John sighed. He was tired. For almost four years, he hadn't really had to think about all of this. He had been numb. He loved feeling joy and happiness, but the feelings he was dealing with now . . . John shook his head. Dealing with his emotions over Sam's death was bad enough, but there was a body count piling up. And, it was time to stop it, regardless of who this madman was. John looked over at Jessica and Chet who had been studying him and gave them a fake smile. Jessica chuckled, and John knew he had been busted.

John climbed into the car without a word. Jessica and Chet followed. Jessica started the car, and off they went to Pamela Davis's home. Chet was working on his phone as they drove. He whistled as he found something.

"What did you find out, Chet?" Jessica asked.

"I just got an email from the psychiatric hospital, showing orders for David George to be transferred. According to the records, David George was checked out by Agent John Fowler. I'll forward you both the email so you can look at it on your phones."

"Why would someone sign David George out as me?" John asked. He then added as an afterthought. "I don't think I can get email on my phone, Chet." Chet shook his head. "Then I'll text it to you, or can your phone not get attachments?" John pulled his phone out of his pocket to look at it. Chet's mouth dropped open. "May I see that?" John handed him the phone. Jessica saw it as they passed it between them.

"I haven't seen that model before, or at least in ten years," she commented. "Is that a retro look, Chet?" Chet didn't answer immediately. He kept looking it over.

"No, Jessica," he replied, somewhat in awe. "I think this phone is over ten years old. I don't think it even receives texts!" John nodded.

"That's what I thought, but I wasn't sure," he replied.

"John, how can you not have a phone that receives text messages?" Chet was on the verge of a breakdown. "How can I know you, and you not have a phone that can do anything?"

"It does something," John responded. "It makes all the phone calls I need."

Chet sat back, shaking his head in disbelief.

Chapter 65

When they arrived at the remains of Pamela Davis's home, John hung back to talk to Jessica. Chet walked past them, still shaking his head.

"Did I do something wrong?" John asked. Jessica shook her head.

"No," she replied. "It's just sometimes, he thinks you two have nothing in common. It's not that you did anything, but you have to understand. That kind thing is his life, and you're his best friend. He feels like you don't think what he does is important sometimes."

"That's ridiculous, Jess," John replied. "I'm the most easily replaceable member of this team." Jessica just looked at him.

"John, you're not," she replied simply. "We've proven that already. You are the heart and soul of this team. And frankly, Chet and I are both good with that. Give him some time. He'll be ok." Jessica patted him on the shoulder and started inside. John stayed behind for a second, thinking.

John realized he knew very little about either of his friends' lives. John knew that would bother most people, but what he did know was that Jessica, Chet, and Trip had his back, no matter what happened. He knew he could count on them for anything. That was all that mattered in John's world. He could just hear Sam telling him that's not how most people worked. It wasn't that he was wrong either. Sam always reassured him of that. But, at the same time, she reminded him friendship wasn't a one-way street. It couldn't always be about him. He had stood there longer than he realized because Jessica had walked back up to him and was giving an amused look.

"Thinking about her, aren't you?" she asked gently. John nodded. "Just so you know, I expect you to think about her." John smiled gratefully. Jessica continued. "Chet's not upset with you. You know that right?" John nodded. Something told him this was one of those times he shouldn't speak, so he was going with it. Jessica continued.

"It's kinda funny," she began, looking at the ground, scratching her head, and then looking back at John. "We were joking one day that if something happened to her, I was going to have a lot of trouble on my hands. She told me that some days, I would have to choose between beating you up and kissing you. I wish I had listened more back then. I wonder if she knew she was going to die." Jessica shook her head. John chose his words very carefully.

"It's not fair," he began. Jessica looked sad for a second, thinking he was referring to Sam. John continued. "You and Chet are always making sacrifices for me. I'm not going to tell you I'm going to change, and I'm not asking you to, but I can be much more understanding." Jessica smiled and began to move toward him to hug him or kiss him. John wasn't for sure because that's when he heard Chet.

"For crying out loud, there's a murder here!" he exclaimed. "Can you two wait until later to have this tender moment?" With that, Chet spun and walked off. Jessica turned to go.

"He needs to switch to decaf," John said where only she could hear.

"He needs to quit drinking those energy drinks," she responded where only he could hear.

"He possibly needs a girlfriend," John said.

"There's no possibly about it," Jessica responded.

"Word," John said. Jessica put her hand out to stop John and turned toward him.

"Don't ever say that again," she said. John started to speak, but she reached over and closed his lips with her fingers. "Never again," she repeated and started into the house.

"I saw it on a movie," he said defensively. Jessica never turned around and kept walking as she answered.
"Never. Again."

Chapter 66

John followed Jessica and Chet into the house. He watched one of the crime techs. The tech was doing something on one of those tablet thingys. John got closer to see it. He had to admit he was impressed. The tech was giving him a weird look.

"I've never seen one before," John explained. The tech looked even more shocked. Chet looked over at him with a look that John could only describe as one a married guy would get if his wife caught him talking to a hot woman. John walked away, head down.

"Really?" Chet asked and walked away in disgust. Jessica was trying to keep a straight face.

"Do you two need a room?" she asked. The medical examiner gave them all a look. Chet and Jessica appeared a little ashamed but not John. He had a look of vindication on his face.

"Was her neck broken?" Jessica asked, trying to get the investigation back on track. The medical examiner shook her head.

"No," she replied. Chet and Jessica were surprised. The examiner continued. "From what I can tell, she was smothered, possibly by this pillow. I'll have to do fiber analysis and run some tests on the pillow." John was nodding, thinking.

"Has she been dead more than four days?" John asked. The examiner shook her head no. John turned to Chet. "You know that thing you tried to email me? Can I see it on one of those thingys?" John asked, pointing to the tablet. Chet gave John a withering look. He walked over to a tech to borrow it from him, muttering under his breath.

"Thingy," he said with disgust as he handed the tablet to John. He showed John how to flip through the document. John flipped until he found what he was looking for. The release paperwork had been started over a week ago according to the date on the paper. He showed Jessica and Chet.

"What does that mean?" Chet asked.

"My guess," John began, "is this murder was not part of the original plan. The neck isn't broken. In fact, my guess is this lady saw the face of the killer when David George was taken from that facility, and that's why she's dead. This raises a couple of questions. One, is this the same killer as the rest? I think it is, but we're not 100% sure. Two, and the answer to this one could crack the case open. What does someone gain by releasing David George? The obvious answer is someone that wants to hurt Archibald and possibly his daughter. Anyone seeing anything here that I'm missing?"

Chet shook his head no. John looked over at Jessica.

"Do we warn Archibald?" she asked. John thought about it and grinned. Jessica and Chet both mocked groaned. Jessica playfully backhanded John in his chest. John headed toward the car with the other two following. He was anxious to get back the headquarters and tell Trip his plan. He was sure Trip would love it.

Chapter 67

John was quite happy on the ride back to FBI headquarters. He had a definite plan that he was sure would lead them to one of Archibald's partners. He was afraid it would be Duck and not Kenneth. John chastised himself internally. He had no actual proof that Kenneth was the third man, but boy, did it fit the puzzle.

"You're going to do something stupid, aren't you," Jessica said, not asked. John grinned. Chet shook his head, chuckling.

"I know it's useless to ask you what you're going to do, but will it upset Trip?" Chet asked. John thought for a minute.

"You know, I don't know," John replied. "He's not the same guy." Jessica nodded in agreement.

"He really began to change when you went undercover," she said in agreement. "You weren't there to see it, but he really went to bat for you, John. He knew you were in too deep. He was trying to get you out to help you, not to punish you." John nodded as he listened.

"He thinks it's his fault for Sam's death," John responded. "I can see it clear as day. Of course, both of you do as well. I just didn't know if he changed because of her death or if something had happened before. I'm beginning to think a lot happened in that time when I was undercover that I missed." Chet clapped John on the shoulder.

"And, they say you can't teach an old dog new tricks," Chet said.

"Who you callin' old?" John retorted.

"Well, you are the SENIOR agent in the car," Jessica responded.

"You're the one dating me," John fired back.

"Because, sadly, it took until you reached this age for you to mature closer to my age," she fired right back.

"I'm not that much older than you!" John exclaimed.

"You act ten years older than all of us," Chet responded. John sat for a second, sulking.

"This could get ugly," he said after a second.

"We're not worried," Jessica responded. "We'll put you in a home when you get too old and ornery." John turned, ready to fight when he saw the playful look on her face. She patted his leg hard. "Calm down, grumpy. We know what you're talking about, and we don't care. We're seeing this thing through to the end."

"A whole lot of people I knew are dead because of this thing," John said quietly. Chet glanced at Jessica. She caught the glance. She looked at John, but he never turned in her direction. Neither she nor Chet knew what to say. John went on. "I just don't want to see anyone else die that doesn't have to. It looks like someone has a personal beef with me, so I should be the one to settle it."

"You do that, and I'll hurt you," she said quietly.

"Jess, I can't stand not having you in my life as my friend, partner, and girlfriend, but if I was to be the cause of your death . . . I don't know if I could go on," John finished in a barely audible whisper.

"First off," she began hotly. "You kill yourself; I'll kill you." John thought about telling her how impossible that was but thought better of it when he saw the look on her face. "Secondly, who said anything about me not being in your life?"

"If I settled this by myself," John replied, a little nervous.

"I said I'd hurt you, not leave you," Jessica replied. "John, you don't get it. We both understand your ancient code of honor. Okay, so we don't understand it. We honestly wonder if the ancient ninja cult you learned it from does," John gave her a withering look as Jessica ignored him and continued. "But, we know this code of

157

honor exists, and it has these rules that only you and . . . well, you . . . no one but you understands these rules, but that's not the point. We want to help you, but we both know that if you decide to go all John Fowler, there is nothing we can do. But, let me point out something. The last time you went all John Fowler on something was the Mafia case. You went in like the hero from an old western, and the fallout nearly killed you. It doesn't have to be that way. There are people in your life John. Sometimes you forget that."

John was very quiet for a moment. He knew she was right.

"You're right about me," John replied softly. Jessica beamed; she was so pleased with herself. "But, you're wrong about me forgetting about people being in my life. After what happened, I can never forget what happens when I ignore someone in my life." The smile fell off Jessica's face. She felt about half an inch tall. Chet was in the back, trying not to let Jessica and John see him wince in pain from the comment. The rest of the ride back to the FBI headquarters was filled with an uncomfortable silence, which ironically, John welcomed.

Chapter 68

They parked in the parking garage of the FBI headquarters. Before John could get out of the car, Jessica turned to him to speak.

"John, I'm sorry," she said simply.

"Jessica, if you apologize every time you mention Sam, you're going to be saying you're sorry a lot. You didn't upset me." John smiled, opened the door, exited the car, and started toward the elevator.

"He just wanted quiet, didn't he?" Chet asked carefully. Jessica was looking more than a little irritated.

"I think he did," she responded shortly. "Sorry, Chet, it's not you I'm irritated at." Chet got out of the car, chuckling.

"The band's back together," he replied as he shut the door. In spite of herself, Jessica couldn't help but smile. John had held the elevator, and all three rode up together. No one said a word, but just before the doors opened, Jessica stomped John's foot. John was still limping as they entered Trip's office. Trip eyed the three when they walked in. He could feel the tension, but at the same time, it was obvious they were back to being themselves. As he watched John limp and hop and saw the self-satisfied smirk on Jessica's face, it was really obvious they were back.

"Say something dumb, John?" Trip asked, already knowing the answer.

"It would appear, sir," John responded, giving a sideways look at Jessica.

"Baby," she mouthed at him. Chet started chuckling.

"Children," Trip chided, trying as best he could to hide his smile. John sat down without being asked. "Do you feel like you're at home?" Trip asked.

"Yeah," John replied. "Yeah, I do." Trip smiled and nodded. That was the thing with John; if you asked

159

him a question, you were going to get an honest answer. He offered the other two a seat and they both took them.

"I have bad news Jessica. Steve and Jeff told us everything they have done wrong since they were old enough to walk. Unfortunately, there is nothing illegal that Archibald has done. Immoral, yes, illegal, no." John was smiling broadly. Trip knew he shouldn't ask, but he couldn't help himself. "What am I missing?"

"You threatened them with Jessica, didn't you? John asked. Trip nodded, and Jessica lowered her head and covered her face. She prayed John wouldn't say anything. Apparently, that prayer wasn't answered as she heard John continue. "See, like a bomb."

"What?" Trip asked, perplexed.

"I told Jessica she's like a bomb. The best thing about having a bomb is the threat of the bomb, not the actual use of it," John explained. Trip had a pained look on his face, and he turned toward Jessica.

"I'm sorry," Trip said simply.

"Right?" Jessica said, exasperated. "Captain Dodo thinks it's a compliment."

"Would you like to be reassigned?" Trip asked. Jessica reached across Trip's table and patted his hand.

"You are such a dear," she responded. "But, no, I think I'll just deal with what I have here. Like Dad said, if life gives you lemons, make lemonade." John was watching the two. He didn't find the humor Trip, Jessica, and Chet did.

"I'm sitting right here, you know," John said. Trip turned and looked at him and then turned back to Jessica, ignoring John.

"You're so strong," he said to her, trying not to laugh.

"I have an idea to trap Archibald, or at the very least to make him do something stupid," John said, trying to get someone to pay attention to him. Trip smiled at Jessica.

160

"I'm sorry, but that is the priority right now," he said. Jessica nodded solemnly.

"I understand," she said. Trip turned toward John with the biggest grin on his face.

"Let's hear your great plan," Trip said, and then after a pause added, "Captain Dodo."

Chapter 69

"David George is loose," John said simply. Trip's smile fell off his face. In fact, Trip looked like he might be having a gas attack from the news.

"Apparently, I signed him out, according to the paperwork at the hospital," John responded. "Haven't you opened the e-text that Chet sent you?" Trip looked at John for a second and turned toward Chet.

"You sent an," Trip paused, looked back at John and then over to Chet. "E-text?" Chet nodded, trying to hold back the laugher. Jessica covered her mouth with her hand to try to cover the laughter she was failing to hold back. Trip checked his computer. He looked up at John, smiling. "Oh, look," he was fighting back a laughing fit. "It's the E-text." John was oblivious. He was sitting in his chair looking quite proud of himself.

"I was thinking that I might go in with one of those hidden ear piece things that you have that we don't like to talk about and tell Archibald what happened with David George, as a courtesy. I was also thinking while I was there, I might, accidently, let him know that he's working for someone," John explained. Trip's face broke out into a slow grin. Jessica shook her head and interjected.

"Wait, Archibald's not working with someone, but for someone? Am I missing something?" she asked, slightly confused.

"No, Jess," Chet said, also smiling. "It's brilliant! We're implying that the most egotistical-"

"Except John," Jessica interjected. Chet smiled and continued.

"Narcissistic," Jessica pointed at John. Chet shook his head and continued. "Self-important," John reached up, grabbed her finger and pulled it down. "Man we know is working for someone else. He'll lose it."

"Not only that," John explained, letting go of Jessica's finger and giving her a scolding look, "he might mess up and call one of the people he's working with."

"So?" Jessica answered. Chet was looking very impressed.

"If I'm right there in the truck, I can track the signal off the cell tower and follow it," Chet began. "Now, if someone uses a prepaid cell phone, we won't know who they are, but we can track their location. It is possible someone could bounce the signal if they knew what they were doing. If they don't though, we might not be able to find out exactly who they are, but we can find out where they are."

"I knew all that TV stuff was fake," John said, knowingly. Jessica fought so hard to not laugh that her eyes started watering. John sat, looking proud of himself.

Jeremiah Cosby
Watergate Apartments, Washington D.C

Chapter 71

Jeremiah Cosby stood in front of the Watergate Apartments and looked up. This building was the heart of the one of the biggest controversies in United States history and had ultimately cost a President his career. If the American people knew what had transpired here over seven years ago, he wondered how many careers would be ended, including his own. Jeremiah almost hadn't taken the meeting, but he had been given the blessing of the man who would be sworn in as President and would have Jeremiah made Vice-President a few days later. Jeremiah thought back to his conversations with John earlier that day. John had been so close to the truth, and Jeremiah had wanted to tell him. But at that time, the soon-to-be President didn't trust John. That's what surprised Jeremiah. He was called tonight, told to come here, and to make his own decision.

Jeremiah pushed the thoughts from his head and started to his destination. When he reached the room he was told to go to, he knew instantly he was in the right place since there were secret service men positioned on either side of the door. They immediately recognized him and brought him inside.

Susan, the former First Lady, saw him, walked over to her old friend, and hugged him.

"Jeremiah, it's been too long," she said. She backed away and smiled at him. "I'm sorry, but we didn't want to put you in any type of situation. That's why you were never told before you agreed to be the Vice-President."
Jeremiah nodded.

"I don't like it," Jeremiah said. "But, I understand why you didn't tell me. We all agreed we needed to end corruption in government!" Susan had a sad smile on her face.

"Kenneth talked me in to it," she said simply. Jeremiah nodded.

"What would he do if the truth came out? What would you do?" he asked quietly.

"What does it matter?" she answered with a shrug. "I'm tired, Jeremiah. He lives the same way every day. I am worn out. What happens if I get sick? It would all come out then if someone had to take care of him." She rubbed his arm. "Don't worry about me. Go see him and decide for yourself."

Jeremiah walked into the other room. Susan could hear the two men talking. She left them alone, and in about 15 minutes, Jeremiah walked out. He looked sad.

"Do you understand?" she asked, and Jeremiah nodded in response.

"Do you know for sure that Kenneth used the same trick?" Jeremiah asked. Susan shook her head no.

"For sure, no," she responded. "But, I have to believe he did when he saw how well it worked," she trailed off. She looked away, gathered herself, and turned back. "The look on his face when he discovered it would work was like a wolf looking at helpless chickens." Jeremiah nodded.

"I still think he has to know," Jeremiah said.

"The FBI agent?" she asked. Jeremiah nodded.

"I don't see the point of telling the country what happened," Jeremiah began. "But, if John can understand what Kenneth did, then maybe he can stop him."

"Do you really think he's capable of such things? Do you think the man that was the President of the United States could do some of the things we've all heard rumored?" she asked. Jeremiah looked her dead in the eyes.

"Don't you?" Susan looked down to the ground, sighed, and then looked at Jeremiah, nodding her agreement. Jeremiah continued. "I'll bring him when I can. It will be a few days, but he has to know."

"I trust you, Jeremiah," she said. With that, she kissed him on the cheek, led him out the door, and closed it behind him. Jeremiah left the building more shaken than he thought he should be. What bothered him the most was how completely everyone had been fooled.

John Fowler
FBI Headquarters, New York

Chapter 72

"When do you plan on executing your master plan?" Trip asked John.

"I was thinking tomorrow morning. Can we get everything together in time?" John asked. Chet nodded.

"We can take the surveillance van down tonight, but someone will have to ride in the back," Chet explained.

"I was wondering if I could go by myself. I need to go to the Moores and have a talk with them," John said.

"Is there something wrong?" Jessica asked.

"No, nothing like that," John responded. "I just need to verify some things with them." Trip nodded.

"Sounds like a plan," he said. "Keep me in the loop. Jessica, do you want me to bring Jeff and Steve to the box individually and give them a scare?" Jessica looked a little disappointed.

"No," she said, almost pouting. "If they've admitted everything, what's the point?" John and Chet exchanged a quick glance and both shuddered. John headed out the door and toward the elevators. He got there and heard someone jogging behind him. He turned, and there was Jessica. She had a quizzical look on her face. She slowed from her jog but continued to walk towards him. John couldn't get the image of a cat toying with a mouse before the cat ate the mouse out of his head, no matter how hard he tried.

"Something wrong, Jessica?" John asked. Jessica walked up to John and placed a hand on the wall right beside him, effectively pinning John.

"I was going to ask you the same thing," she replied very quietly. "Why are you going back to the

Moores?" John sighed and tried to find a way out of this predicament. When he decided he couldn't find one, he decided to go with something that was on his mind, but not the main reason he was returning to the Moores.

"You," he said simply. Jessica looked confused. "I'm not saying anything is going to happen with me or you, but if it should someday, I want to make sure there aren't any problems."

"What are you talking about? Marriage?" she asked, very confused. John tried to blow the question off.

"What? Marriage? No, well, I mean, maybe. Why? Do you want to?" John was about to have a nervous breakdown. He thought maybe he picked the wrong reason to tell Jessica. Jessica backed up. John took a deep breath.

"Look," he began. "When two people begin dating, one possible outcome is marriage." John paused, making sure she was with him. "I'm not saying I'm wanting to ask, today, tomorrow, or next year, but if I did, I need them to be ok. I know this sounds stupid, but after all we went through. I want to make sure they aren't going to resent you." Jessica looked at him for a long minute. No one, and she meant no one, but John Fowler would worry about such things. She sighed and tried to speak calmly.

"You're being absolutely serious, aren't you?" she asked. John nodded. "It's going to bother you until you do?" John nodded again. "Then, by all means, go." John smiled, gave her a kiss on the cheek, and turned to hit the elevator button. "What if they do have a problem with it?" she asked quietly. John winced. He hadn't considered that. He also realized it was a good thing she hadn't seen him wince because she might have taken it the wrong way. He said a quick prayer of thanks that he was facing away from her. John turned around, took a deep breath, and began.

"If I decided I wanted to marry you, I would. They could have the money back. As long as I tried, Sam would be happy," he replied.

"Money?" she asked. John looked confused. "What money?"

"You didn't know?" he asked. Jessica shook her head no. "Oh, I got all of Sam's money when she passed." Jessica had never considered that before. She smiled at him.

"So, what, a couple of thousand dollars?" she asked as John waited for the elevator. John barked a laugh. The doors opened, and he stepped in.

"No," he said like she was an idiot.

"A couple of hundred thousand?" she asked, trying not to appear too inquisitive.

John snorted another laugh. "You really don't know?" He held the door open and looked up and down the hall. He leaned toward her and whispered. "I think it's a little over a hundred million." He leaned back, and the doors slid shut. Jessica stood there mouthing the words "a hundred million" over and over.

"Then, why were you a private investigator?" She asked the closed elevator door. The door never responded.

Chapter 73

Jessica headed to the foxhole. John had given the basement the name since most of the agents that had been stationed in the basement had dug in like they were in a foxhole, fighting for their careers. The three of them decided to take over the foxhole to end the anxiety agents had when they were assigned there.

Jessica walked over to Chet who was doing something on his computer. Jessica really didn't care right then. They needed to have a talk.

"Chet," she said, skipping pleasantries. "Does John really have a ton of money, and if he does, why did he work those awful jobs when he was gone from the FBI?" Chet turned to look at Jessica. He smiled.

"You just found out, didn't you?" he asked. Jessica nodded.

"I had the same reaction," he continued. "I took him a freelance job when we needed help within the agency, thinking he could use the money. He would have gladly done it for free. It's his brain. It just constantly needs something to solve." Chet shrugged. "It's who he is." Jessica looked a little irritated. "Have you bought him dinner or something?" Jessica glanced at him sideways, set her jaw, and nodded. She looked down, a little ashamed. "You know it doesn't occur to him."

"That doesn't surprise me," she replied. "I think things not occurring to him is the norm, not the exception."

"Have you tried talking to him?" Chet asked. Jessica gave him another sideways glance, clearly irritated.

"He literally just told me as the elevator doors slid shut," Jessica replied. Chet clapped his hands and nearly feel out of his chair laughing. Jessica walked into her office, grabbed her overnight bag, and came back out; Chet was still laughing.

"Come on, laughing boy," she said dryly as she headed out of the foxhole. Still chuckling, Chet grabbed his gear and followed behind her.

John Fowler
The Moores

Chapter 74

John had taken a little longer to get to the Moores' residence than he thought it would. He had stopped at a phone store to upgrade after the incident in the car earlier. The guy at the store had spent a good thirty minutes trying to explain to John how to use the phone. John had understood less than 10% of what he was told. He had finally gotten the guy to give him an instruction booklet. John had to look up the definition of booklet because the booklet that was given to him was thicker than many phone books he had seen.

John was sitting in the Moores' drive, trying to think of exactly what he was going to say to Arthur and Madeline. Honestly, he wasn't too worried about them. He was worried about Jessica. He loved Jessica, but he didn't know how to convince her of that. He didn't even know when he was allowed to tell her he loved her. John dropped his head onto the steering wheel. He knew he should probably be having this conversation with Jessica, but he wasn't sure she would understand. John hadn't exactly lied to Jessica. He didn't want there to be any problems between the Moores and Jessica, but what bothered him was why him? John knew that both Jessica and Sam deserved the best in the world, so why him?

Arthur and Madeline were standing at the window watching John in the car. Rosa joined them.

"What is he doing?" Rosa asked.

"My guess," Arthur answered, "is it's got something to do with Jessica. Knowing John, he either wants our permission to marry her, or he needs advice, or both." Rosa looked confused. Madeline smiled.

"Rosa, when John came to ask us for permission to marry Sam, Sam had to warn us a month before he actually came," Madeline began. "The boy came to our house every couple of nights, and sat in our driveway. After about thirty minutes or so, he finally decided he couldn't do it and drove off." Rosa looked even more confused.

"He lived in New York then?" she asked. Madeline and Arthur laughed.

"No," Arthur replied. "They didn't move to New York until after they married. It was about a two hour drive roundtrip for him though."

"So, did he ever ask you if they could get married?" Rosa asked. Madeline smiled at the memories, and Arthur continued to chuckle.

"One evening, Sam brought him over her," Arthur began. "She drove, kept the car keys, and wouldn't let him go until he asked me." Arthur smiled and turned toward Madeline. "Do you remember when she drug him in the other room and what she told him?" Madeline nodded.

"She told John that she didn't care what we said, that she would marry him," Madeline began. "But, John had to ask for our permission."

"Why was he so scared?" Rosa asked. Madeline's smile changed. It was a sad, sorrowful smile, and Arthur turned away.

"He thought he wasn't worthy of Sam," Madeline said softly. Arthur gave a sigh that sounded like a bear growling.

"Well, the boy was weird," Arthur said, trying to defend himself. He turned and looked at Madeline. Madeline gave him a look that left no question about how she felt about that comment. "Well, he was," Arthur insisted.

"But, no one ever loved her more, and it was her choice," Madeline replied.

"And, no one ever made her happier," Arthur admitted. "But, she was my little girl, and I wanted something wonderful her."

"Like Kenneth?" Madeline asked. Arthur grumbled.

"He did grow up to be the President of the United States," Arthur said, trying to defend himself again. Madeline just stared at Arthur for a minute. "Go out there, and bring the poor boy in," she ordered. Arthur didn't argue. He went outside, opened John's door, and dragged the protesting FBI agent into his home.

Chapter 75

John was surprised by Arthur. He was even more surprised when he half-drug him into his home. John tried to protest, but Madeline joined Arthur, and they both stood there, smiling knowingly.

"John," Arthur began. "It's fine with us if you marry Jessica." John stood there with his mouth open. "That is why you're here, right?" John wasn't sure what to say.

"Well, it's what I told Jessica," John began. He saw Arthur and Madeline's face and hurried with his explanation. "But, that's not really why I'm here. I mean, if I was to ever propose to Jessica, then I would want your blessing, and that's great that I have it now." John saw the confusion on their faces. He sighed. This was really one of those times he needed Sam. "The real reason I'm here is I need your help." John wasn't sure how to ask what he needed to know, so he just blurted it out. "Did Sam pick me over Kenneth?" Madeline's face gave John the answer he needed. Arthur looked away. "So, she did," John said quietly.

"She didn't love him, John," Madeline replied. "They only dated because of who they were. She often told me she didn't even like him, and she wasn't sure she trusted him." Madeline led him over to the couch. "You need to listen, John. When she met you and called home from college, I had never, ever, heard her that happy in her life."

"How?" John asked quietly. "I mean, let's be honest. He's loaded, powerful, charismatic, and even I have to admit he's easy on the eyes." Madeline chuckled at the last part of John's comment. Arthur walked over to him. He had been listening from across the room.

"John, this isn't easy for me to say," he began. "She picked the better man when she picked you. There's something about Kenneth." John knew what he thought about Kenneth, but hearing these two that had known him so long only strengthened his belief that he was involved, somehow.

"I need to ask the two of you something that I know you don't want to talk about, but it's crucial to the investigation," he said as gently as possible.

"I think it was him," Arthur said quietly, looking at the floor. Madeline looked at Arthur sharply. "I mean, I can't say in front of a room full of people that I think the ex-President of the United States raped my daughter, but looking back, I think it was him."

"That's why you don't want me to exhume the body," John said quietly. Arthur nodded. Madeline stood up and walked over to Arthur.

"You never told me," she said simply.

"Why upset you?" Arthur asked. Madeline nodded sadly. John shook his head, disgusted.

"Why is everyone so scared of this guy?" he asked.

"Who's everyone?" Arthur asked. John winced. He had let that slip and didn't mean to. "Jeremiah?" John nodded. Arthur sighed. "There have been rumors that Kenneth knows some sort of secret or holds something over a lot of people. As to what that is, I don't know." Arthur walked over to the mantle and looked at a picture of Madeline, Sam, and him. He turned back to John. "I tell you what, John. You find something in your investigation and need that body exhumed, and I'll do it." Madeline stared at Arthur for a second, and then nodded.

"Fair enough," John responded. "Now, I have a favor to ask. May I spend the night here?"

"You know you can, John," Madeline replied. The three talked for a while, and then John turned in, knowing he had a big day the next day. He was going to poke a very big bear with a very sharp stick.

176

Bruce Cosby
Kenny Kline's Club

Chapter 76

"I was afraid of this," Bruce said to no one. He was waiting outside of Kenny Kline's club. He was growing impatient. He knew John was stupid and slow, but this was just ridiculous. Bruce was ready for the endgame to happen, but John was too busy being a proper investigator. Bruce had to admit he had not thought of John thinking Archibald had anything to do with this. Well, no one killed Sam but Bruce, but he had been given the idea by two different people. Something occurred to him.

"I wonder if they played me?" he asked to no one. Bruce thought about it, decided it didn't really matter, so he let it go. Bruce sat up in his seat. Someone was heading into the club. It was one of Kenny's meatheads, not Kenny himself. He could give the message to one of the meatheads, but he was sure they were much too dumb to repeat it verbatim. He was quite sure they couldn't even spell verbatim. Bruce wondered if John could spell verbatim. Bruce shook himself. He took another gulp of his energy drink. He hadn't slept in over 48 hours. He was beginning to think that maybe he was getting a bit silly. He couldn't sleep though, not until John was dead. He was positive John would figure out that he needed to go to Kenny's club by tomorrow, and this would all be over tomorrow night. If not, he could just break into John's apartment and beat him to death with a tire iron. That would go against the plan, but at this point, he was beginning to not care. All Bruce wanted was John dead.

Bruce saw Kenny pull up, get out of his car, and enter his club. Bruce smiled and picked up the stupid hat in the passenger seat. It resembled the hat that John used to wear all the time. He was enjoying pretending to be John, so why not one more time, just for giggles. Bruce got out of the car, locked it, and headed into the club. Soon, it would all be over.

Archibald Staples' Mansion
Virginia

Chapter 77

As John pulled up to the gate, he realized there was a major problem with his plan. He didn't have a warrant. One of Archibald's goons, they all looked alike to John, stopped him and asked for his identification. The goon took his ID and made a call on a phone inside the booth by the entrance. A few minutes later, he returned to John.

"Here you go, Mr. Fowler," the goon said. "Mr. Staples is at the firing range behind the house. Just pull up to the house, and someone will walk you to the range. Have a nice day."

John drove up to the house and was met by a large group of Archibald's men. John smiled as they approached him to try to pat him down. He pulled out his FBI badge and slowly shook his head no. The goons looked confused. One of the more intelligent members of the group said something into an earpiece. After a few seconds, he waved John to continue on inside. John followed the men around the house to a shooting range that had been built in the back. Archibald saw John and smiled. He was curious as to what had brought John to his home.

"John," Archibald began. "It's so good to see you again. What brings you to my humble home?"

"You shouldn't lie like that, Archibald," John retorted. Archibald chuckled. "I came to warn you that someone has freed David George. I thought it was my duty since they used my name to do it." Archibald chuckled over the news. He already knew that David George was free. It amused him to no end that his sources had more timely information than the FBI.

"Well, John, I have to thank you for informing me of this," Archibald said. "If there is nothing else, I have much to do today." Archibald turned around and reached for a new weapon. He had many different weapons out, test firing different ones as he saw fit.

"A most impressive collection of firearms, Archibald," John said. "Do you think we could have a few minutes alone? The goons didn't look very happy with that suggestion. "The other option is I could call in a team, and we could start checking for permits for these weapons." The goons liked that idea even less. Archibald looked mildly irritated.

"Leave us," Archibald said. The group of heavily armed men left. Archibald turned to John.

"Mr. Fowler," Archibald began. "I suggest you be very careful. I sent the men away so they won't report you to the FBI when you make some wild accusation about me like you did when you were here a few days ago and took my housekeeper. You should know that my hospitality only lasts so long." John smirked at Archibald and picked up one of the handguns.

"I'm guessing this is therapeutic for you, Archibald. It must be nice to fire a weapon here, since you never get to do any of your dirty work yourself," John said as he looked over the weapon. Archibald's eyes narrowed; John continued. "You make sure there's never anyone who can be tied to you don't you, Archibald?"

John aimed the gun at the target and glanced over at Archibald.

"Haven't you ever just wanted to do your own dirty work once in your entire life?" John asked quietly. Archibald twisted his neck until it cracked. It seemed to John that Archibald was a little uncomfortable. John grinned; he was about to turn the pressure up to 11.

"Of course, that would surmise that you are the one who's in charge," John said as he lowered the weapon and turned toward Archibald. "Maybe you're the one who's being led around by the nose. Maybe the great Archibald Staples isn't the biggest dog in the yard like he wants everyone to believe." Archibald scoffed.

"John," Archibald began defiantly. "I have no idea what you are talking about, but let's just say that I did. Why would I ever let someone rule over me, or even attempt to use me?"

John was doing a dance internally. He had taken a stab based on something Rosa had said earlier, and it appeared she was right. It was time to go big or go home.

Chapter 78

"You know I have partners," John began. "But, at the end of the day, everyone assumes I'm in charge of my team. I'm man enough to know that I couldn't do anything without them." John held the gun out away from Archibald and looked down the sight as he continued. "But you, Archibald . . . you think no man controls your destiny. You're wrong. You think you have partners, but you're wrong. You're not their partner; you're their underling. Well, maybe you're the #2 man."

Archibald's nostrils flared, and he decided he had had enough of John Fowler once and for all. He started to reach for a gun when suddenly he felt the muzzle of the gun against his face and heard the gun being cocked. Archibald swallowed; he knew he had gone too far. John slowly started to turn, which made Archibald turn. They continued until Archibald's back was to the firing range targets. John smiled.

"I would love nothing more right now than to arrest you for attempting to draw a weapon on me, but we both know that you'd beat that charge in no time." John's smile turned angry. "I know you had something to do with Sam's death, Archibald," John said very quietly. Archibald tried to hold his cool, but he swallowed. John knew. It was so clear. Everything in his mind screamed Archibald had something to do with it. He could end this right now. John knew that Archibald didn't pull the trigger, but he was the reason it was pulled. No, that wasn't exactly right. Archibald was working with someone else; in fact, John wasn't so sure that Archibald's strings weren't really being pulled by this mysterious partner. John thought about asking if it was Kenneth Nichols but decided to keep that nugget of information to himself, for now.

John knew he could end Archibald here and now and probably get away with it. He could yell out for Archibald not to go for the weapon and then fire, saying he was shooting in self-defense. He also knew that wouldn't bring back Sam, and more importantly, it would let the other members of Archibald's little cabal off the hook. He needed Archibald to bring the other two down. He knew he couldn't shoot Archibald, but Archibald didn't know that.

"You know, Archibald," John began. "I could do the world a favor and blow your head off." Archibald gulped noticeably. John stepped back a little, gun still trained on Archibald. "The problem is you're a little fish." Archibald looked like he was about to come unglued.

"She got exactly what she deserved!" Archibald spat. John grinned. That was just the opening he was looking for. John's arm flinched, and he fired.

Chapter 79

Archibald dropped to the ground like a sack of potatoes. John rolled his eyes at the sight.

"Wow," he said. "To be the big, tough guy you're supposed to be, you act like a drama queen." Archibald looked up at John with pure hate in his eyes. John squatted down and grinned at the sight. Archibald placed his hand over the ear the bullet had gone by. John was sure Archibald was at least temporarily deaf in that ear. John looked down at the target. He couldn't see for sure, but he thought he had hit the bullseye. John looked back down at Archibald.

"I'm going to bring you and your buddies down, Archibald, if it's the last thing I do. Do you hear me? YOU'RE GOING DOWN!" John paused and then spoke very softly. "You tell your buddy and whoever you two had kill Sam that their days are numbered. I'm going to get the killer, and then, I'm going to end your little empire. After that, I'm coming to get your boss." John stood, turned, and began to leave. Archibald's face was red with anger.

"John, I'm going to kill you!! Do you hear me!! I'm going to see you die!!!" John kept walking but answered.

"Careful, Archibald," he replied. "I could have you arrested for threating a law enforcement agent."

"YOU'RE GOING TO DIE!!!" Archibald screamed. John chuckled and spoke very quietly.

"Do you think I pushed enough buttons?"

He listened and heard Jessica's voice come through the tiny receiver in his ear.

"That was either the greatest thing I've ever heard or the dumbest," she replied.

"It was pretty dumb on his part," he replied.

"John, I was talking about you," Jessica said with concern in her voice. "You have just riled up one of the biggest criminals I have ever seen."

"Alleged, Jessica, alleged," John said, trying not to smile. He had reached his car. He got in, started the vehicle, and headed off the estate. "Does Chet have anything yet?"

"Not yet," Jessica replied. "We have eyes on him, and he's screaming at everyone. Wait. He just got handed a red cell phone. I think we may have something. Get to the van; Chet's at work."

John smiled. Bingo, I've got you now, Archibald.

Chapter 80

John raced over to the van. He jumped out of the car, opened the back door, and bounded inside. Chet was smiling and shaking his head at John.

"You do know this doesn't happen just instantly, right, John?" Chet asked. John looked over at Jessica who had a big grin on her face.

"I know you just don't gaggle it," John said. Jessica looked at John with surprise on her face. Chet was trying to hold in the laughter. Jessica prodded him.

"He thought you'd just 'gaggle' it," Jessica replied, trying to hold in a laugh. John wasn't sure what they were finding so funny. The look on his face caused Jessica to burst out laughing. Chet continued to smile as he worked.

"John, a computer is not a group of geese," Chet said, holding in his laughter.

"Are you two trying to tell me the term is not 'gaggle'?" John asked. Jessica was laughing so hard John thought she was going to need oxygen. John was getting a little annoyed at these two. He started to say something when Chet yelled out.

"Gotcha!!" Chet exclaimed. His excitement diminished quickly though. Chet shook his head. "He's good," Chet said softly. He turned in his seat and looked at his friends.

"Sorry, guys," Chet began. "I traced the call and thought I had him, but he's wicked good. The signal leads to 1600 Pennsylvania Avenue." John let out a low whistle. He couldn't believe it! It had actually worked! They had Kenneth Nichols! Jessica shook her head.

"No, John," Jessica said, laying her hand lightly on his arm. "It's not like that. Somehow, he avoided Chet's signal and made him think it was coming from the White House."

"Or, Archibald has someone in the White House," John countered. He couldn't believe these two didn't see it.

It all made perfect sense. Jeremiah and Trip kept insisting that the whole thing was too big for them. What was bigger than the White House? John was ready to fight his two friends on it when he saw the look on their faces. John thought for a second. He knew nothing about computers, tracking cell phones, or even texting for that matter. If his two friends assured him he was wrong, then he had to take their word for it. He needed more proof that Kenneth was involved. He couldn't reveal his conversation with Jeremiah, and without that, he had nothing. Honestly, Jeremiah had never actually admitted it was Kenneth.

John could just hear Sam chastising him how they were supposed to be a team, not John and the Fowleretts. . . except this was bothering him. He had to wait until there was something substantial he could take to Chet and Jessica. He needed time and proof. These thoughts took John less than a second. He nodded to his friends.

"You two know better than I do," John said, effectively giving up the fight. "We'll just have to go about this another way." His friends nodded. John looked back at Archibald's mansion. John knew Archibald, Duck, and Kenneth were involved; it was just a matter of time before he proved it.

1600 Pennsylvania Avenue
Red Cell Phone

Chapter 81

Tom sat in his office, thinking about his friend Luke. Tom had warned Luke about staying away from the First Lady, but his obsession with her had eventually cost him his life. Tom glanced over at the red cell phone to make sure it hadn't vibrated. It hadn't. Tom couldn't ever remember a time when it did. Tom was so excited when he had gotten assigned to the Presidential detail, but so much of it had been relegated to him watching the red phone.

He still didn't know how the former President pulled off having one person watch the phone 24/7, but he knew better than to ask. Kenneth Nichols knew something that got him anything he wanted, anytime he wanted it. That was saying something, given all of the things other Presidents had known. What made Tom even more upset was the fact he had been assigned to remain with the soon-to-be-former President when he physically left the White House, which was any day now. Kenneth had resigned that morning, and his Vice-President had just been sworn in. Kenneth was taking his time leaving. Honestly, who could blame him? He was walking away from the most powerful job in the country, not an easy thing for anyone to do.

Tom jumped in his chair. It wasn't possible, but it had happened! The phone was vibrating. Tom answered like he was supposed to. The man on the other end was furious. Tom asked him to wait a second, and he called into his earpiece that the red cell phone was active. He rushed through the White House to find the President. Tom stopped at one of his secretary's desks, showed her the phone, and was immediately buzzed into the Oval Office.

Tom walked in and handed the ex-President the red cellphone. The President nodded at Tom. The former President signaled to everyone packing up the room to leave. Tom turned and left the room, followed by everyone else. The ex-President stood, went to the window, and spoke.

"This is Kenneth," he calmly said.

"Did you tell Fowler? Why?" Archibald hissed.

"Archibald, have you lost your mind?" Kenneth asked. "What do you mean did I tell Fowler?"

"He was here today, saying how I take orders from someone. First off, I take orders from no man! We come to decisions as a collective! Secondly, how could he know!? If you haven't been talking, then that means it was Duck!" If Kenneth didn't know better, he'd think that Archibald was foaming at the mouth.

"Archibald," Kenneth said calmly. "I just had to resign and watch someone else be sworn in to do the job we worked so hard to get. I am moving out of this office right this second, and you call me about this? You need to calm down. All he's doing is grasping at straws. You do realize you may have made a mistake by calling me?"

There was silence on the other end of the line. When Archibald spoke, he was much calmer.

"He's much better than I gave him credit for, isn't he?" Archibald asked. Kenneth chuckled.

"As much as I loathe that man, he is one of the best detectives around," Kenneth admitted. "We need to end this."

"Agreed," Archibald said. "May I?"

"I thought no man controlled you?" Kenneth asked simply. Archibald chuckled.

"No one does, but I do understand that sometimes it is best to consult others," Archibald answered.

"If Bruce fails in his quest, then you have my full permission. Duck has always said we can take him out whenever the two of us think we need to," Kenneth replied.

"Thank you, my friend. I'm sorry for my outburst. Will I see you soon?"

"Think nothing of it. I have a few things to finish up, and then, I will vacate this office," Kenneth looked around as he answered. "It's a shame David George just didn't shoot Fowler right here." Archibald roared with laughter and disconnected. Kenneth broke the phone in half in his hand. He buzzed his secretary. She walked in, and Kenneth simply handed her the pieces. She left, taking the phone to be completely destroyed. She shut the door behind her, leaving Kenneth by himself.

"I have something, John," Kenneth said very softly. "Something that you can't take from me, no matter what you do. I win, you poor fool, and you didn't even know we were playing a game." Kenneth went to his desk and picked up the phone.

"Ruby," the ex-President said into the phone. "Call my special number." The President waited for the other end to pick up.

"I'm coming home soon," Kenneth said simply as the person on the other end answered. He was ready to move on with his life with his special girl.

Chet, Jessica, and John
Surveillance Van Outside of Archibald's Estate

Chapter 82

Chet was rechecking the call, and Jessica was working on the computer. John wasn't 100% sure what either was doing, but he thought back to the conversation he had had with the Moores. Jessica had said to him he could try harder to understand people. Something suddenly started to make noise and vibrate in his pants pocket. Jessica slowly turned to look at John with an eyebrow raised. John smiled an embarrassed smile.

"New phone," he said as he pulled out the smartphone. Chet glanced at it and then did a double take. It was the newest model available. Chet didn't even have one yet. He let out a low whistle.

"Nice, Boss!" Chet said, nodding in appreciation. "Do you know how to use it?" John shook his head slowly. Chet took the phone from John and glanced at it. He smiled. "Its charge is low. That's why it's making all the noise and vibrating. Do you want me to charge it up and fix the settings on it?" John nodded. Chet started to play with it for a second and jerked his head back in surprise. He looked over at Jessica. She glanced at the phone for a second and then at John.

"John, did you know the person at the phone store signed you up for some different social media sights?" Jessica asked. She was prepared for John to throw a small fit. She was surprised at his response.

"Actually, I did that," John replied. Jessica and Chet were floored. They took a second to recover. John went ahead, not noticing their shock. "I was thinking that maybe we could check some social media sites and possibly get a lead on the case. I've read notes on other cases where that was the big break. I don't know a lot about the sites, but I'm pretty sure we could check Thwapper and FaceSpace and see if we could get some leads." John realized he was rambling and looked down at the ground, trying to collect himself. He was so out of his element talking about anything electronic. He didn't understand any of these things, but he knew he needed to make an effort, for Chet's sake. John was blaming himself for the position Chet had placed himself in while John was on the Mafia case, and he thought he needed to do something to connect with Chet.

While John was avoiding Jessica's and Chet's gaze, they were trying to collect themselves. As soon as John looked down, Chet mouthed the word, "Thwapper?" At the same time, Jessica mouthed the word, "FaceSpace?"

Jessica got up, walked over to John and took his hand. He looked up at her. She was looking at him, concerned. "John, that's a good idea, but it doesn't work that way. People have to post on those sites about things they have done, and we know that Archibald is much too secretive to do things like that. I would also think that as long as this little group we're chasing has been together, they would know better than to as well." John had a resigned look on his face. He was afraid it was a stupid idea. He knew he really had no clue what he was talking about. Chet was tapping his finger on the computer desk, thinking.

"Actually, maybe it's not," Chet said. Jessica turned; a look of astonishment was on her face. Chet ignored her. "His men might tweet something, or even the guy we're chasing might. Archibald has a lot of goons, and it only takes one to mess up. IF the guy we're after is supposed to be like Archibald, he's a megalomaniac. If they think they've fooled you again, he might not be able to resist bragging about it. I could search for keywords," Chet paused, knowing he was about to lose both of them. "It's a long shot, but it's not bad, John, not bad at all." John beamed. He turned toward Jessica smiling. Jessica simply put her hand in his face and pushed him away. Chet smiled. "John, do you think you could find the cord that came with your phone, and I'll get it straightened out." John nodded, still beaming. He turned to Jessica, promptly stuck his tongue out, and left the van. Jessica shut the door behind him.

Chapter 83

"Chet," Jessica began. "Why did you lie to him?"

"I didn't," Chet replied, never looking up from his work on the computer. "It is a huge long shot, but it's not out of the realm of possibility." Chet stopped and swung around in his chair. "What was that about Thwapper, and FaceSpace?"

Jessica held a hand up. "Chet, he got two halves right of social media networks. For him that's as good as one." Chet smiled. "Thwapper?" He began to chuckle. "What do you do, thwap someone?" Jessica was trying not to burst out laughing. "I'm guessing he feels guilty?" Chet asked, trying to turn the conversation serious. Jessica nodded, trying to get the grin off her face. Chet nodded, thinking. "I guess I'm going to have to talk to him."

"Oh great, another night of you two drinking orange sodas and arguing over where the three point line should be," Jessica said. Chet shrugged.

"I believe in the international three point line," Chet replied. Jessica snorted.

"You only watch basketball every four years in the Olympics!" she retorted.

"Have you told him about your MMA obsession yet?" Chet asked. Jessica shook her head.

"I'm not for sure how he'd feel about a girlfriend who enjoys seeing guys break each other bones." Chet smiled when she referred to herself as John's girlfriend. Chet thought for a second and decided it was time to clear up things between them.

"Well, I guess this is as good a time as any," Chet began. Jessica looked at him questioningly. "I'm sorry for using you."

Jessica tilted her head and grinned at Chet. "You did blow it," she replied. Chet grinned at her. "I guess if I'm being honest, I'm sorry for using you too. I went out with you to find out about John. I know I could have just asked, but . . ." Jessica trailed off. She shrugged, and Chet smiled at her.

"For the record," Chet began. "It was my favorite assignment that Archibald gave me." Jessica laughed out loud as John entered the van. He paused, worried he had interrupted something. Chet held his hand out for the cord, and John handed it to him. He looked at his two friends, sighed, and spoke.

"I really had no clue what I was talking about earlier, did I?" he asked, feeling more than slightly embarrassed. Jessica, standing to John's right, turned her head slightly to her right where she didn't have to look at John, and where he couldn't see her fighting back a smile. She ran her left hand through the side of her hair and along the back of her neck. John nodded and started to leave the van.

Chapter 84

"Wait, John," Chet said. John stopped and turned back. "I wasn't just shooting smoke earlier. That idea of yours was good. There's little chance that it will work, but it wasn't a bad idea." John nodded and looked down at the ground. He looked back up at Chet.

"I'm sorry, Chet," John said. Chet looked a little surprised. "I don't know how to do small talk. I don't know how to talk about stuff I don't care about, and I don't know how to fix what I messed up while I was gone. I'm talking about while I was drunk, not physically gone." Jessica put her hand on John's right shoulder, trying to comfort him. John swallowed and continued. "If I had been there, you wouldn't have done what you did. I'm sure of it, Chet. I let you down, and I'm sorry. I spent the last little bit trying to learn this stuff, and even went and got a new phone . . . which the cost is ridiculous by the way!" Chet stifled a laugh. John smiled and went on. "I needed a phone that could . . . . oh what's the word." John took a second to think of what he was trying to say.

The whole time Chet was silently repeating over and over, "Don't say thwap; don't say thwap; don't say thwap." John snapped his fingers, and Chet brought his attention back to John. "I need to be able to text," John said. The look on his face said he wasn't 100% sure he had used the right term. Chet smiled and nodded. "Chet, I'm sorry. I want to make this right, but I don't know how."

Jessica squeezed his shoulder and rubbed his arm. Chet smiled at his friend.

"John, it's ok," Chet replied. "What happened was my fault." John started to reply, but Chet held up his hand. "John, I'm a big boy, and I got in bed with Archibald. I knew what I was doing, and I did it anyway. It's my fault, not yours." Chet was silent for a second and then continued. "We're good, John. You don't have to keep trying to learn about my world." Chet held out his hand,

and John shook it. John started to turn when Jessica came up behind him and whispered into his ear, "I'm proud of you for trying. Thank you." John smiled at Jessica, and Chet went back to working on his computer. John went out of the van with Jessica following him.

"What's our next move, John?" Jessica asked. John thought for a second. He was pretty sure that what he wanted to do, Jessica wouldn't let him. He wanted to go back to Washington, D.C. and talk to the President, but he was sure that would be voted down by everyone. He scratched his head, thinking. He had an idea, but it wasn't one he liked.

"Do you have something to wear for dancing?" John asked. Jessica looked at him incredulously.

"I'm confused," she confessed. "Are you asking me out on a date? Because if you are, I'll go if dancing if that's what you want to do, but I was talking about the case."

"So am I," he answered. Jessica looked very confused. "It's not that I wouldn't like to take you out, it's just . . . well, I can't dance and . . ." John put his hand over his mouth, blew into it, and then pulled his hand down his chin, rubbing it. "Let me try again." Jessica was very amused. "There's this guy named Kenny Kline. He used to know everything about the underworld. If someone bought it, stole it, or sampled it, Kenny knew about it. He's the one guy that I could approach that hasn't been found dead yet in this investigation. He's got this club that's supposed to be popular, so I thought you and I could go to it." John looked down at the ground, wondering if he had messed up. Jessica reached over and gently lifted his head.

"I'd love to go, even if there wasn't a case," she replied. "Don't worry; we'll have fun. I promise."

"The place probably won't be up and going until nine or so," he replied. Jessica gave him an amused look.

"Later?" Jessica nodded. John dropped his head. "Midnight?" he asked hesitantly.

"Do you have a curfew or something, John?" Jessica asked. John shook his head no.

"You know me. I'm just an old fuddy-duddy that thinks I should be at home at that hour," he replied.

"You are an old fuddy-duddy," Jessica paused. "I can't tell you the last time I heard someone use that world."

"Leave it to me to bring up ancient history," he replied. "My place, 11:30?"

Jessica smiled, nodded, and headed toward her car. John took a deep breath. He got in his car and began the drive back to New York. He spent some time on the road, thinking about Kenny Kline. John wondered how he had avoided the massacre that had claimed so many that he knew in those days when he was undercover. He saw a convenience store on his way and all he could think about was how the last time he was at a club like he was going to tonight he was drunk as a lord. John realized he was thirsty, pulled over, and headed inside to get something to drink.

Chapter 85

Jessica arrived at John's apartment around 11:00. She was concerned that John might be in a bad place. With all the killings of people in his former life and what he had learned about Sam, she decided to get there early and see if he wanted to talk. To be honest, she wished she had ridden back with John. She wasn't sure that John being alone for that long was a good thing.

Jessica realized she had been standing in front of John's door thinking about him and the past. She took a deep breath, started to knock, but changed her mind and opened the door to John's apartment. She was wearing a long coat since the nights had turned cooler than normal for late March. Jessica expected John to be ready. John had always lived by the motto to be 15 minutes early is to be on time. To be on time is late. She was surprised that he wasn't. John sat on the couch still dressed in his normal suit she had seen him in earlier that day. His tie was loosened, which was odd. Typically, John took his tie off any chance he got. In front of John sat a bottle on the coffee table. Jessica sprinted across the room to grab the bottle. John saw Jessica and tried to smile at her, but his heart just wasn't in it. Jessica grabbed the bottle and looked at it. According to the label, it was tea. Jessica took the top off and sniffed it. It was tea. She looked at John, apologetically. John now smiled, amused.

"John," Jessica began. "I'm so sorry. I know going through Sam's case file and seeing all these people that had something to do with your time undercover has been very hard on you. I saw the bottle and I thought-" Jessica paused, knowing there was no good way to say what she had been thinking. "John, I'm sorry. I thought you had fallen off the wagon"

John chuckled. "You saw what looked to be a bottle of alcohol in front of an alcoholic who has been going through some of the most painful memories in his life. You did what anyone would have done; you got ready to chew me out." Jessica looked slightly embarrassed. John got up and headed toward the kitchen. "That's always best, if you didn't know; chew out someone who's down on himself and trying to lose himself in a bottle." Jessica gave him an exasperated look and followed him into the kitchen.

"Is that something you learned in AA?" Jessica asked. John had opened the refrigerator and had his head stuck in it. He pulled his head out and looked sideways at Jessica.

"No, that's just something from the Fowler playbook," John replied.

"Is that why you don't have a sponsor?" Jessica asked. She had wanted to ask him for the past few days why he never had a sponsor and thought now was as good a time as any. As she asked the question, she began to slip her coat off. Underneath, she was wearing a red, tight, low cut dress that ended mid-thigh. John kept his head in the fridge to answer her and didn't notice her outfit.

"It took me almost four years just to speak at a meeting Jessica. I am not a poster child for AA. I'm not saying my way is right, but for me, it has worked so far," he paused, finding the container he was looking for. He opened it up and pulled out a leg of chicken. He continued to speak while closing it. "I imagine one day, it will come back to bite me, but I just couldn't share some of the things concerning Sam that are inside me. I know I should have, and when this thing is over, I probably will, so-" John finished closing the container, pulled his head out of the fridge, and began to shut the door. "Until then, I'll have to use you as. . .my. . .good brown gravy," he whispered at the end. John had finally noticed Jessica's outfit, and the chicken leg fell out of his hand and bounced on the floor of the kitchen.

Chapter 86

Jessica smiled at John whose mouth was open.

"I'm going to take it that you approve?" Jessica asked. John nodded, his mouth still open. Jessica reached over and closed his mouth for him, grinning.

"Uhh, we're supposed to be undercover," John managed to spit out.

"Do you think any guy is going to be able to describe my face?" Jessica asked. John thought for a second. He wasn't sure if this was a trick question or not. He finally decided it wasn't, shook his head no, and attempted to breathe. Jessica nodded at him and continued. "Women won't really be able to describe my face either. They won't be paying attention to you. They'll be too busy saying nasty things about me and describing how I'm dressed to their friends." John gulped and nodded. Jessica slowly started to walk toward John. She pushed him back against the wall behind him. John's eyes were wide open.

"As for being your sponsor," Jessica continued. "I only know of one way to do things, and that's tough love. That's the Hammerstein playbook." John nodded. "See, here's how it works. If you don't drink, I do this." Jessica kissed John deeply. John saw fireworks in his mind. For a second, he realized he forgot to breathe. Jessica broke the kiss and moved her lips a few inches away. She continued. "If you do drink, you don't get that, understand?" John nodded vigorously. Jessica patted him on the cheek, turned, and walked out of the kitchen.

"Wait!" John yelled. Jessica looked back over her shoulder. "I haven't drunk in almost four years. Shouldn't I get more of a reward?" Jessica smiled and headed back into the living room, putting on her coat.

"You men," she began. "Always wanting a reward for what you're supposed to do." John followed her into the living room and sat down beside her.

"You're a mean lady, Ms. Hammerstein," John said. Jessica smiled at him and began removing his tie. John lifted an eyebrow, and Jessica smacked it. "Ow! What was that for? I didn't do anything."

"Maybe," she replied. "But, you were thinking about doing something." John shrugged and smiled.

"Exactly why are you removing my tie?" John asked.

"We need to go to the club and find your source, Kenny what's-his-name," she replied.

"I can't go Jessica. I just can't go," John said, looking down at the ground.

Chapter 87

"Oh, for heaven's sake, John!" Jessica exclaimed. "Put your big boy pants on, and quit whining!" John looked at Jessica in shock. Jessica shook her head, looking perturbed.

"I mean, if it's not one thing, it's another," she said, straightening his clothes until she decided that he was ready. "What is it this time that has you down in the dumps? What about this place reminds you about Sam that you can't handle?" John's mouth was open in shock. She reached up and closed it for him. "Shut your mouth, you big baby, before you catch flies."

"It has nothing to do with Sam," John said silently, still looking stunned. Jessica got an embarrassed look on her face and began arranging the two magazines on the coffee table.

"Is there something you'd like to share, Jessica?" John asked quietly. Jessica was quiet for a second, and then, she shared.

"Have you ever thought how impossibly tiring it is to hear you go on and on some days?" she asked, slamming one of the magazines on the coffee table. John involuntary flinched at the sound of the magazines hitting the table. "Sam this and Sam that. I'm scared of this, and I'm scared of that." She looked John straight in the eye. "John, I . . . care about you deeply." John had started to look surprised when she nearly slipped with her words. She ignored him and continued. "But, I need a man who wants me, and not because I'm available, and his true love isn't here any longer."

John nodded. He looked straight ahead, not sure what to say. Well, he knew what to say. The problem was he wasn't allowed to, and he didn't think Jessica would believe him right now. He reached out and took her hand without looking at her. He turned back with tears in his eyes.

"You know, you're right," John said. "I do go on and on sometimes. I know I sometimes act like I'm the only person who lost someone. I know I need to do better about that, and I have tried. But, Jessica, as for the other . . . how do I convince you I'm with you because I," John paused. Jessica stared at him, daring him to say it. John gulped. "Care deeply?" Jessica nodded. John nodded and went on. "About you, and I want to be with you and only you?" Jessica looked at John with a sad look on her face. She pressed her lips together and shrugged.

"I don't know, John. That's something you need to figure out," she replied.

"Something I need to figure out?!" John exclaimed. Jessica nodded. "That's unreasonable, that's crazy, that's . . ." John let his sentence trail off. Shock covered his face.

Jessica shrugged and grinned. "Take it or leave it, John. This is who I am, and this is how I feel." She looked at him, almost challenging him.

"Ok," he answered.

"Ok what?" she asked.

John smiled and shook his head. "OK, I accept your challenge," John said. He leaned in and kissed her on the forehead. He pulled her close and held her. "I accept you how you are, crazy as you are, and I will try to prove to you that you're the only person that I want in my life."

Chapter 88

John held Jessica for several minutes. He didn't want to let go. For the first time in a long time, he felt happy and content. He thought he might feel guilty about it, but found he didn't. After a few minutes, he sighed. He knew they had work to do, so he broke the embrace. He looked at her and decided to tell her his problem.

"The way I see it, we have two problems tonight," he said. Jessica arched an eyebrow. "One is where are you going to put your weapon? And, two, I can't dance."

Jessica smiled and patted John on the leg.

"One, who says I don't have it on me already? And, two, you big baby, I know you don't know how to dance," she replied as she got up off the couch and began to head to the door. John watched her walk away. Jessica turned around and saw him watching. "Are you checking me out, Mr. Fowler?"

"Where?" John asked. Jessica smiled broadly.

"Where what?" Jessica asked innocently.

"Where's the gun?" John asked.

"Come on," she said, ignoring him. "We need to get this over with so we can have you back in bed by a decent hour." John made a ha-ha face at her, got up off the couch, and headed toward the door, continuing to try and spot a weapon. As he approached the door, Jessica stuck a finger directly in his chest. "And, one more thing, Mr. Fowler, if you get any fresh ideas about patting me down, you'll pay for it." John smiled and opened the door to Jessica as he bowed deeply. Jessica laughed and headed out the door into the hallway.

They went down to Jessica's car and headed to the club owned by Kenny. After several minutes, they arrived at the club. John was very nervous about the whole situation. It had been years since he had seen Kenny. Kenny and John didn't exactly see eye to eye in John's days as an undercover agent. Kenny always believed in "sampling" the merchandise: be it drugs, girls, stolen items, or whatever it was Kenny was selling. The thing was Kenny knew everything there was to know in the criminal underworld. Kenny always kept his secrets unless he was selling them.

Jessica tapped John on the shoulder. John came back to the present and looked at the line that snaked around the block. They both got out of the car. John turned to Jessica.

"Don't worry. I'm on the list," he said. Jessica almost burst out laughing. John looked exasperated. "For once, can you trust me?" John started toward the doorman. Jessica took her coat off and pitched it in the car. She locked the car up and followed John. She got there just in time to hear the exchange between John and the doorman.

"I'm on the list," John said.

"There ain't no list, bra," the doorman replied.

"Tell Kenny that John Fowler is here," John said. The doorman crossed his arms.

"No," the doorman replied. John put his hands into his pockets and pushed his tongue into his bottom lip. Jessica decided she had had enough. She stepped out from behind John where John couldn't see her. She got the doorman's attention. The doorman smiled, and his eyebrows lifted when he saw Jessica. Jessica gave the doorman a playful wave. The doorman nodded slightly. Jessica smiled, pointed at John, and mouthed at the doorman, "He's with me."

John noticed the doorman's attention and turned to look behind him. Jessica was still standing there, but she was examining the buildings down the block while scratching the back of her head. John knew she had done something, but he wasn't for sure what. He turned to look at the doorman who was smiling and nodding knowingly.

"You know, Mr. Fowler," the doorman began.

"Save it," John said and started in. The doorman stepped aside and let John and Jessica into the club. Jessica winked at the doorman as she walked by. The music was loud and was nothing that John recognized. Jessica bopped along to the music as she walked with him. John was looking everywhere for Kenny. Jessica smiled and decided it was time to have a little fun, no scratch that, a lot of fun. She grabbed John and led him out to the dance floor.

Chapter 89

Jessica led John onto the dance floor, which was quite like leading a lamb to slaughter. John didn't know the last time he had been in a dance club and paid attention to the music and what was going on. He was watching people dance, and Jessica was watching him. Jessica thought John's eyes might bug out of his head. She was enjoying this. As Jessica was dragging him, she heard a lot of, "Jessica, are they?" "Jessica, is she?" and her favorite, "Jessica . . . is that legal??!?"

She found a spot where the two of them could squeeze in and began to dance with John. John stood like a stone statue. She took his hands in hers and looked into his eyes.

"Follow my lead," she said simply.

"Follow what lead?" he asked, slowly getting flustered and frustrated.

"Just follow me," she replied, looking into his eyes. John let go and slowly began to dance to the music. Jessica watched him and smiled broadly. Whatever kind of dance he was doing wouldn't win any awards, but it was passable to anyone who glanced at them. In fact, compared to some of the other things some guys were doing on the dance floor, it may have ranked in the top half of men dancing in the club. Jessica began to smirk as she realized John was trying to listen to the words of the song. As she saw his eyes widen, she knew she had to get his mind off the music.

"Jessica!!" he exclaimed. "Are they saying what I think they're saying!?!"

"I know, John," Jessica replied. She really hoped that she didn't roll her eyes, or if she did, it was too dark for John to notice. "I am personally appalled by the lyrics the artist chose, but you can report them to the proper authorities later. We need to focus on why we're here. Do you see Kenny anywhere in the club?"

John shook his head no. He hadn't really been looking for Kenny. For John, it was like gawking at a car wreck in the room. Everywhere he looked, he couldn't believe what he was seeing: the clothes, the dancing, the flat out grinding people were doing with each other. John didn't think any of the wildest parties he went to in college could touch the sights around him. He was trying to decide exactly where one couple began and ended when he noticed a huge man walk into a door on the far side of the club. He was pretty sure it was Leo, one of Kenny's guys.

John leaned in, pointed, and told Jessica what he had seen. She nodded and began to lead him through the sea of bodies to the doorway. When they got there, they looked around, saw no one, and stepped inside. Inside the door was a table with Leo and two other huge men playing cards. The looks on the three men's faces told John and Jessica they weren't welcome. In fact, John thought they were about to get thrown out of the club.

Chapter 90

"I've got this," Jessica whispered to John. John smiled and let Jessica take the lead. He knew this would be most entertaining. He leaned back against a shelf and wished he had popcorn to watch the show. Jessica walked toward the table. When she reached it, she placed her hands on the table and leaned forward. John put his hand over his mouth to conceal his laughter. He knew Jessica was, "using what she was given," as she liked to say. John was impressed at how the men tried to conceal their stares.

"My friend and I are looking for Kenny," Jessica said.

"Never heard of him," Leo said, never raising his gaze up to Jessica's eyes. John was impressed the man had even paid attention to the question. Jessica straightened back up. Leo did nothing to hide his disappointment.

"Oh, that's a shame," Jessica said. "My friend John and I were hoping to speak with him." Leo looked over at John. John waved. Leo looked John up and down. Leo rubbed the stubble on his face. John thought that Leo might be having a thought, and the thought was very close to causing Leo's brain to explode or causing him to have a stroke.

"John Fowler?" Leo asked.

Uh-oh, John thought.

Jessica smiled her best smile. "How did you know?"

Leo got up and walked over to John and looked him up and down. He shook his head. Johns swore he could see smoke coming out of Leo's ears from all the thinking Leo was doing.

"This don't make a lick of sense," Leo said. Jessica raised an eyebrow.

"This looks like the guy I used to know a long time ago, but I thought he was dead. The other thing that doesn't make sense is someone claiming to be John Fowler

210

was in here earlier."   John nearly leaped with that revelation.

"This guy, did he smile, and when he did, did you think that's what a snake would look like if he smiled?" John asked. Leo nodded and snapped his fingers toward John. He began pointing excitedly as he spoke to John.

"Yeah, yeah," Leo said, still nodding. "It was creepy." Leo looked at John for a second. "How come you ain't dead?"

"Duck said I was to be left alone, or did you not hear, Leo?" John asked.

Leo threw his hands back in a defensive posture. "Look, if Duck says you're to be alive, then you're to be alive." Jessica looked at John questioningly. John shook his head no where only she could see it. John didn't know if what he said was true before he said it, but it had always made the most sense. Duck didn't want anyone with Mafia ties bringing down John because that would lead back to the undercover Mafia investigation that John was a part of. It might also lead to the Duck's downfall if anyone was to find out what happened between him and Chet; of course, it would lead to Chet being fired from the FBI.

While John was thinking this, Leo was cracking his knuckles. John knew this room was seconds from being a warzone.

Chapter 91

Jessica walked over to Leo and ran her hand over his, stopping him from cracking his knuckles.

"So, Leo," Jessica said playfully. "Are you going to let us in to see Kenny?"

"Lady," Leo said, looking her up and down. "I'm sure you're used to getting what you want, whenever you want. I know you got a whole lot of places by using your," Leo put up finger quotes as he spoke, "skills." John placed his hand over his mouth again to keep from laughing out loud. "But, around here, that doesn't get you much except a good time with a real man, if you know what I mean."

John slid his hand from his mouth to over his eyes, and finally though his hair. Here we go, he thought.

Jessica smiled at Leo.

"I'm sorry, Leo," Jessica began. "I'm not for sure what you mean."

Walk away man, walk away from it, was all John could think to himself over and over.

"See," Leo said, as he began talking to his boys. "All looks and no brains, there's only one thing this one here is good for." Leo's partners were having a good laugh. John had his right hand over his closed eyes. He opened his eyes and spread his fingers so he could see through them. Jessica looked over at John and winked. John shook his head. Jessica began.

"So are you guys saying that a girl that looks like me can't be smart? That she can't work her way up the ladder with hard work?"

"Baby, you completely misunderstood what I said. What I'm saying is that the only work you did was hard work to make it up the ladder. You know what I'm sayin' fellas?" Leo replied. Leo's buddies where hooting and giving high fives for that one. John groaned silently. He knew things were about to get bowling shoe ugly.

Jessica walked up real close to Leo. She ran her finger down his chest. Leo smiled, but it quickly faded as Jessica quickly brought her knee up, directly into his groin. Leo doubled over, groaning. John sprang to the thug nearest to him. He caught the thug with a hard right. Meanwhile the other thug went to grab Jessica from behind. She drove her elbow into his solar plexus and then dropped down and flipped him over her back. The thug started to get up, and Jessica kicked him right in jaw. He dropped in a heap. The thug that John hit had spun around. John grabbed him from behind, twisted the thug's arm behind him, and held him down against the table. Jessica blew a strand of hair that had come loose during the fracas out of her face. John looked down at Leo.

"Think maybe we can see your boss now?" Leo nodded at John and groaned. Leo turned his head when Jessica tapped him on the shoulder and got met by a right cross. He crumpled onto the floor. John looked at Jessica, perturbed.

"Really?" John asked. Jessica looked at John with exasperation.

"With what he just said to me, he's lucky that's all I did," she replied, as she opened the door on the far end of the room. John nodded and let go of the thug he was holding, who slid onto the floor. As John left, he turned back toward the three men.

"Thanks, guys," John said as he exited the room. "She's probably mad at me because I had to take down one of you."

Chapter 92

John went through the same door as Jessica. The door opened up onto a long hallway. Jessica had her gun out and was quietly creeping down the hallway, pressed up against the wall. John stopped and scratched his head. He was still wondering where she had hid the weapon. Jessica looked back and saw John. John signaled her to wait and caught up with her.

"Let me handle this part," John said. Jessica didn't like it, but she nodded and relented. John put his hand over the gun she was holding and pushed it to where it was pointing at the floor. "We won't need that," he said simply. Jessica really didn't like that idea, but she nodded. She didn't holster the gun. John waited for a second. She gave a slight smile and flicked her hand telling John to go on. John smiled back and headed down the hall having been busted on trying to see where Jessica had been holstering the gun.

John reached the end of the hall. He tried the knob on the door, saw it was ajar, pushed it the rest of the way open, and walked into the office. He saw Kenny sitting behind the desk at the end of the room. Kenny smiled when he saw John.

"Saint," Kenny said, referring to John. "I knew that guy wasn't you earlier."

"How's it going, Kenny?" John asked, walking further into the room and up to Kenny's desk. "It's been a while."

"I'd say," Kenny replied. "I thought you were dead."

John smiled and replied, "Duck says that I'm off limits, but the FBI didn't really trust him so they let that rumor make its way around. I didn't really care who knew if I was dead or alive. I mean I've been on TV since then. You didn't see?"

"That thing about the First Lady on TV was you?" Kenny asked. John nodded. "I thought that was you. You know some guy's running around impersonating you?" Kenny thought about what he said and shook his head. "Let me correct myself. Not impersonating, more like saying he was you. In fact, he all but admitted it to me earlier."

John's face fell, and he sat in a chair across from Kenny's desk. All the clues, the wild goose chase, and now he finally had it confirmed; Bruce was running around saying he was John. While all of this didn't mean Bruce was a murderer, it did cast some suspicion on him. Jessica looked at John, knowing that this was killing him. John believed that those who served in law enforcement, of whatever kind, had a special bond. This news hurt John, but more importantly, it should help pull the blinders from John's eyes where Bruce was concerned.

"I heard about that, Kenny. That's why I'm here," John replied, absentmindedly playing with a globe on Kenny's desk. "Was the guy a little bit high strung, with piercing blue eyes, and when he smiled, you felt a little sick inside?"

Kenny nodded. "John, man, I've run with some bad men in my time, you know that. Some of them had real evil intentions, but this guy . . . this guy made my blood run cold. John, he's stone cold." John looked at Kenny, sizing him up. There was no doubt in John's mind. Kenny believed Bruce to be a killer, and John was starting to believe it, too.

Chapter 93

"Kenny, do you believe this guy could have killed a couple of women and men in cold blood?" John asked. Kenny laughed.

"Not only do I believe he could do that," Kenny began. "I believe he could do it while whistling happily. Dude . . . he's whacked."

John nodded. "You said he admitted to you that he wasn't me." Kenny nodded.

"Man, at first, he started off saying he was you, and then, he quit, and just started . . . chuckling." Kenny shivered. "I'm telling you, John. It was the creepiest thing I ever saw. We saw some guys who enjoyed their work, but they had some line that they wouldn't cross, you know, women, children, something. But this guy, this guy . . . it's not there." Kenny looked away for a second. He seemed very shaken just talking about Bruce. He got it together after a few seconds and continued. "Anyways, he says to me that it's obvious that I know that he's not John, but I'm important. I have the answers that John's looking for." Kenny paused and looked down at his desk.

"Go on," John urged.

Kenny's face was a little ashen. If John didn't know better, he would have thought that Kenny was scared.

"He said that he had all the answers that you've been looking for and that he can help you sort through the confusion you feel right now. He said that he will talk with you, where it all started, but alone."

John nodded and sat for a moment. John thought about the note in Ricardo's pocket. It had said "where the rat was found." He thought both places were the same place. He wasn't completely sure though because part of his memories were foggy, for a lack of a better word. John had trouble remembering a lot of specifics about things that happened while he was undercover. John had an idea, but he would need to check a file in his closet at home to

216

verify. While he was thinking, Jessica came over and placed her hand on John's shoulder. John absentmindedly rubbed her hand.

"Did he say where that was, or was he crazy enough to admit anything to you?" John asked.

Kenny shook his head. "Dude, that's so freaky. He said you'd ask that. John, he said he didn't do anything, and it was time for you to confess." Kenny paused a second and leaned in like he was telling a secret. "He said he was ready to hear it."

"What does that mean?" Jessica interrupted.

Kenny threw his hands up. "Lady, I got no idea what that freak show means."

John stood up. "Thanks, Kenny." He held out his hand, and Kenny shook it. "By the way, sorry about your boys out there."

Kenny smiled and waved it off. "It does those mooks some good to get cut down every once in a while. They listen better after a good beat down." His face turned serious for a second. "Saint, watch this guy. I know you've seen some sickos before, but this one . . . where a soul and a conscience is supposed to be in a guy . . . he ain't got either."

John nodded, and he and Jessica exited the office. Jessica turned to face John.

"So now where, Saint?" she asked smiling.

John grinned back at her. "I have no idea," John lied.

Chapter 94

Jessica and John left the club and headed toward the car. Jessica drove back to John's apartment, while John sat in the passenger's seat thinking. Jessica knew John was trying to put together the pieces, but she was worried that there were some pieces he could never find. While John had all of his memories of what happened during his time undercover, she knew some of them were hazy at best. It was obvious to her that Bruce was leading John somewhere, but John seemed to have no idea where. What bothered Jessica the most was she didn't see the normal signs out of John that his mind was working on the problem. It seemed more to her that he was brooding.

They reached John's apartment building, and John got out of the car without saying a word. He seemed to be on autopilot, not noticing anything around him. Jessica followed him upstairs and into his apartment. Jessica was getting the feeling he didn't even know she was there. She sat down on the couch where John normally sat, hoping that would get his attention. John was rummaging through a box in his closet, and after a few seconds, he pulled out a file. He walked over to the couch, never looking up or noticing his surroundings. He stood over the couch like he was about to sit down, right where Jessica was sitting.

I don't believe it, she thought. He doesn't even realize I'm here. At that moment, John started to sit down. Jessica panicked and yelled out, "John!" John was startled. The file went flying out of his hands, and he tried to step forward to avoid sitting on Jessica. He managed to clip the edge of the coffee table. This sent him into a tumble across the floor. John came to a stop flat on his back looking up at the ceiling. Jessica ran over to him and knelt down beside him.

"Are you ok?" Jessica asked. John turned to look at her and quickly snapped his head back around and looked at the ceiling. "What's wrong?" Jessica asked.

"Jess, you probably shouldn't be down on the floor like this in that dress," John replied, never averting his gaze from the ceiling. Jessica gave him a withered look and offered him her hand. John waved her off and came up to a sitting position. Jessica sat down on the couch. She was worried. She wasn't sure she had ever seen him like this before. She thought she might have once, right after Mark Glass was killed.

"I'm not about to drink," John said, as if reading her mind. "I'm just trying to remember some things."

"What things?" Jessica asked. John sighed and shook his head.

"I don't know," he replied. John picked up the case file he had been leafing through when he took his tumble. "I was hoping something in here would spark a memory, any memory that I had forgotten." John paused. He looked out the window at the New York skyline. He turned back to Jessica. John looked sad and depressed. "Forgotten may not be the right word. Drunken stupor or haze might be better." John snorted a breath. "I guess passed out on the floor might be the best way to describe me."

"Hey," she said softly. John shook his head.

"I'm not about to do something stupid. I just hate that what I did all those years ago may keep us from the answers." He looked out the window again and then back at her. "I need to be alone for a bit if you don't mind."

Jessica looked very concerned. "I don't know if that's a good idea." John raised an eyebrow suggestively, and Jessica reached for her shoe to throw at him. John held up his hands defensively. Jessica stopped and looked at him seriously. "I don't know if I've ever seen you like this. I'm worried about you, John."

"Don't trust me?" John asked with a grin.

"No, John, I don't. Not when you're in this condition," she replied, looking serious. John started to get up.

"Listen, you go home, and get some sleep," he said. "I'm too wired. I'm going to stay up all night and work on this. When I get to the point I can rest, I'll go to bed. I'll call Trip and tell him what I'm doing. You come over tomorrow evening or afternoon. I'll make you the dinner I promised: John's homemade pizza." Jessica smiled. "We'll spend tomorrow afternoon or night going over what, if anything, I figured out. If you stay here, all you'll do is fall asleep while I work on this case. We both know that." Jessica grinned ruefully. "I can't believe sleeping in that dress would be comfortable."

Jessica stood up and paused. John nodded and waved her away. Jessica raised an eyebrow. John thought for a second and waved her over to him. She grinned, walked over to him, and began to kiss him but stopped with her lips inches from his.

"Remember the rules?" Jessica asked. John grinned broadly. Jessica kissed him. She broke the kiss.

"Don't do anything stupid," she said.

"I always do something stupid," he replied. Jessica turned and walked toward the door. She opened it, paused, and looked back at John.

"Like getting me to leave you by yourself in this condition?" she asked.

"Jess," John replied. "I'm not going to drink."

"I know," she replied. "This may be the one time I wish you would."

John looked stunned. "What do you mean by that?"

"If you were drunk, then all you would do is sit around all night and blame yourself that Sam's dead, or cry, or get into a shouting match with me," she began. "It's when you're stone cold sober like this that I know you're planning something. John, you're out for revenge."

"You can't be too sure about that," John said. "You haven't asked me to promise you I wouldn't."

"I don't want you to lie to me," she replied. "Good-bye." With that, Jessica walked out the door and shut it. John stood there, nodding.

"Maybe I finally did teach her how to read people," John said to no one in particular. He swore he could feel Sam in the room, shaking her head.

Chapter 95

Jessica walked out of John's apartment building and got into her car. She really wanted to storm out, but she wasn't for sure what good it would do, and she knew she'd look stupid to someone walking by. She looked up at his window and saw him on the phone. She supposed he was talking with Trip. Her mind thought back to the Moores' home when she thought she had seen Sam.

"There's a day coming soon that he is going to choose between me and you, and I want you to know that I'm rooting for you," Sam had said to Jessica. Jess shook her head. That wasn't Sam; it was her subconscious. It had to be. Jessica didn't believe in ghosts. Neither did Sam, which would make the whole thing very ironic. Jessica did recall a conversation that Sam had reminded her of. The two had once promised if one of them died before the other, then the one who died had to come back and watch over the living friend. Jessica pushed those thoughts from her head. She felt like fighting, even if no one else was there, and the thought of someone watching over the other was too warm and fuzzy for her right now. She was irritated and wanted to get it out of her system.

"He's still picking you over me, Sam," she said out loud to no one. Jessica hit the steering wheel with her hand in frustration. She drove off and tried to find a song on the radio. She laughed loudly when she found her and Sam's favorite song. Part of her wondered what John would say if he knew. It was one of those oldies that John always listened to. Jessica and Sam used to tease John relentlessly about how he hadn't heard a song in the current decade.

Jessica listened for a second, decided she was too mad at Sam to listen to it, and changed the station. Jessica stopped the car in the middle of the street. It was late at night, but that action got her a host of inappropriate hand gestures and names hurled at her from the other drivers around her. There was the song again. Jessica was staring

222

at the radio. She flipped back over to the original station. The song was in a different place in the arrangement. Jessica sighed. It was just a coincidence . . . or was it. Jessica's heart was racing. She checked a third station, and there was their favorite song again. She swore she could hear Sam singing loudly to it, off-key as usual. She looked around the car, but she was by herself and didn't see Sam anywhere.

Jessica blew out a breath and did a U-turn in the street. She raced back to John's apartment. When she got there, she noticed the lights were out in his apartment. She cursed herself for not waiting earlier to see what he was going to do. She raced across the street and hurried up to his apartment. When she got to the door, she didn't even bother knocking. She used the key Sam had given to her in case of emergencies to open the door. If this wasn't an emergency, she didn't know what qualified. She flipped on the lights and saw a folded piece of paper on John's coffee table with her name on it. She crossed the room, picked up the paper, and opened it. It read simply:

Jess,

I guess I picked Sam over you again, but this is something I have to do on my own. It's my fault what happened to her, and I have to make it right. I hope you can understand and forgive me. This is the last time I pick her over you, I promise.

Love (Yes, I meant to write that)
John

Chapter 96

Jessica grabbed her phone and began to call John. John's phone rang on his end. After five rings, the computer voice came on the phone.

"Hi, Hotstuff," the voice on the other end said. "John can't come to the phone right now." Jessica stared at the phone.

"The idiot can't figure out a text, but he can name my contact, Hotstuff?" she muttered as she called Trip. She got him on the phone and quickly told him what was going on. He told her to stay where she was, and he would come to her. Jessica disconnected, quickly called Chet, and told him what was going on. Like Trip, he told her he was on his way. They both told her they were only a couple of blocks away. Apparently, they were at the same karaoke bar, and neither one knew the other was there. If Jessica had time and wasn't so upset, she would have laughed out loud. Jessica hung up and scanned the apartment, looking for the files that John had been reading earlier. They were nowhere to be seen.

Jessica thought about waiting for Chet and Trip but then decided against it, went to his closet, and started looking through it. She found the box of files John had been looking through earlier. On the box, written in marker, was the word Sam. She pulled out the box and brought it over to the coffee table. She started thumbing through the files and was shocked. Inside were files on every person the FBI had wanted to bring down in the undercover Mafia case, plus Ricardo Antony. Jessica had no idea which file John had been looking at earlier. She searched for a file on Kenny Kline and couldn't find anything. Jessica was becoming frustrated.

"Blast it, Sam!!" Jessica screamed. "He's going to get himself killed just for you . . ." Jessica thought back to what she thought Sam told her. "There's a day coming soon that he is going to choose between me and you, and I want you to know that I'm rooting for you," Jessica put her hand to her mouth. That's what Sam, or Jessica's subconscious, or whatever she was, meant.

Jessica was becoming hysterical. She was trying to get control of herself. She put her hand on her forehead and ran her hand through her hair, nearly pulling it. She had to get control of herself. There was no proof that this was going to get John killed. It was just her runaway imagination; that was all. Those thoughts worked for about a second. Jessica screamed at the top of her lungs.

"SAM!!!! Why won't you help me!?!? He's going to die!!!!" And with that, Jessica grabbed the box of files and flung them across the room where they crashed into a wall. The box ripped open, and the files went flying everywhere. As Jessica was breaking down, Trip and Chet opened the door to witness the box flinging. They all three watched one file. It seemed to come down slower than the rest. It landed on its back, opened. Jessica quickly crossed the room and picked up the folder. It was opened to a picture of the bar, This Thing of Ours.

This was the bar the group had discussed earlier at the Moores' home. The former owner of the establishment thought it would be funny to open a bar named after the English translation of Cosa Nostra. He didn't find it nearly as funny when the mob turned it into their personal hangout. FBI and law enforcement agents all saw the irony. More importantly, this was where John was first approached by the Mafia and began his undercover work. The bar was abandoned now, one of many companies to go out of business after John's big bust. No one would go into the bar since it was a known Mafia hangout, and all of the Mafia members that use to frequent it were either in prison or relocated. Jessica looked up at Chet and Trip. She handed them the folder and ran toward the door.

"What's going on?" Trip demanded.

Jessica barely slowed. "We're going to save John's life, and then, I am going to kill him!" With that, Jessica was out the door. Chet turned to Trip who was shaking his head.

"This is why no one wants agents to date," Trip replied. Both men hurried after her.

John Fowler
This Thing of Ours Bar – New York

Chapter 97

John stood outside the boarded up establishment with a host of emotions running though him. This was the spot where he began his greatest work accomplishment and his greatest failure. It was here that the foundation had been laid for bringing down members of the Mafia. It was also here the foundation was laid for him to become an alcoholic. John shook the memories from his head and walked around to the back of the building. He saw a door was ajar. He reached into his coat pocket and fidgeted with the device inside it. After he was satisfied that he had done things correctly, John pulled his gun out and opened the door. It was pitch black inside. He saw a light switch and flicked it on, not thinking. A few lights came on. John was surprised, and realized he probably shouldn't be.

John slowly began to search the establishment but found no one. John was sure this was where he'd find Bruce. John felt bile climb up his throat at the thought of Bruce being behind all of this. John had finally accepted that it could only be Bruce behind everything after they had left Kenny's club. John hated to think it, but the evidence was overwhelming. John wasn't sure what he was going to do. Part of him had always sworn he was going to kill whoever had killed Sam, but this was the Senator's son. Jeremiah would probably forgive John for killing Bruce, but what if he didn't? Moreover, John wasn't a cold blooded killer. As much as it hurt John, he knew he had to bring Bruce in alive.

John's eyes wandered to some pictures that were on the wall of the bar. He recognized many of the figures in the pictures. In fact, he found himself in a couple. John was troubled that he didn't clearly remember some of these moments. How drunk had he been back then? He started to turn as he felt something hit his back. He began to spasm violently. In a few seconds, it was over. John was on the ground, unconscious and twitching.

Bruce walked up behind him with his stun gun.

"Sorry, buddy," Bruce said to John's unconscious form. "I may have juiced this one up a little too much." Bruce began to giggle and then broke into a full laughing fit. When he finished, he whistled merrily as he handcuffed John to the bar and began the final stages of setting up his master plan.

"Life is good," Bruce said to an unconscious John. "It's a shame I've got to end yours."

Chapter 98

John awoke with a pounding headache. He sat up and looked around. He had been lying across the counter while sitting on a barstool. How he hadn't fallen off the barstool he had been sitting on he had no idea. John couldn't remember what had happened to him. He looked around. The building was deserted, but John recognized it. He was in the same bar that the Mafia had approached him in five years ago. Why was he here?

John went to feel his head with his hand, but found he was handcuffed to the brass pipe that ran the length of the bar. John looked around the building. Dust covered the tables, and chairs were on top of them. The only thing that was clean was the bar he was sitting at. He took a second look at the far corner of the bar. John noticed a figure leaning back in the corner holding a bottle. It was Bruce. Things were slowly starting to come back to John. Bruce had left a message with Kenny to meet him where it had all began. There had also been the message left on Ricardo Antony's body. John looked down at his pants and noticed they were wet in the crotch. He hit me with a stun stick or stun gun, John thought.

Bruce walked up to John. Bruce was tapping the bottom of the bottle with his hand. John stared at it; he recognized the bottle. It was a special drink that Sam had custom made for him at a local winery. They were supposed to drink it the day he closed the big Mafia case. She had personally made it and told him there was something special she was supposed to tell him that night. John's mind was spinning. He hadn't thought about the bottle since her death. It was obvious now that Sam was going to tell him that she was pregnant. Something was nagging at John; why would Sam make him a wine? She hated John's drinking, and a few days ago, Sam's mother had let it slip that Sam was pregnant the night she died. John silently rebuked himself again for not noticing that which had been right in front of him. John was supposed to be a great detective, and he had missed the signs that Sam was pregnant.

Bruce sat the bottle down on the bar right in front of John, snapping him back into the present. Bruce reached into his coat and pulled out the cloth bag he had been carrying. Bruce opened the bag and pulled a ring out of it. A sick smile covered Bruce's face. He laid the ring right beside the bottle. Bruce softly said his little rhyme that had become a tradition.

"If I had a sister, I wouldn't miss her."

John's mouth went dry. He was trying to focus on the ring, but his eyes couldn't. John's stomach wanted to explode. That was Sam's wedding ring. That was the ring John had put on Sam's finger during the wedding ceremony when he had asked Sam to be his wife. How was that ring here? John couldn't think straight.

John looked at Bruce. There was a red haze that seemed to surround Bruce in John's sight. John used his free hand to check and see if there was blood covering his eyes, but there wasn't. John was so furious that he was literally seeing red. No, furious wasn't the right word. John was entering a whole new level of mad. Worse than that, John wanted a drink, badly. Bruce opened the bottle he had been carrying, poured a shot glass full, and placed it in front of John. John looked at it for a second. He knew what drinking that drink would do. He looked Bruce right in the eye. Bruce grinned at him, a sick, evil, sadistic grin. Everyone had been right; Bruce had killed Sam, Thelma, Dr. Freeman, and who knew how many other people. John could smell the drink and smiled inside. Sam, he thought, forgive me for what I'm about to do, but it's the only way. He reached out, grabbed the drink, and didn't hesitate. He drank the shot in one gulp and slammed the glass down in front of Bruce.

"Hit me again."

Bruce roared with laughter. He filled John's glass again.

Chet, Trip, and Jessica
Racing to This Thing of Ours Bar

Chapter 99

Jessica was driving like a speed demon. Trip and Chet were hanging on for dear life in the car. Trip wasn't sure which he was more worried about, crashing into something at over 100 mph or Chet hurling on him.

"Jessica," Trip began. "While I appreciate the seriousness of this situation, have you thought about what you're going to do once we arrive? If we arrive," he added under his breath.

"Yeah," Jessica replied. "I'm going to put all the bullets I currently have in my gun into Bruce, and then, I'm going to get another clip and empty that one into him. After that . . . Mr. Fowler and I are going to have a serious come to Jesus meeting."

Trip began to answer when he noticed Chet was looking a funny shade of green. "Jessica!" Trip yelled. Jessica saw it and pulled over. Chet rolled down the window and began to empty the contents of his stomach. Jessica got out of the car, while Trip chased after her trying to talk to her. Jessica cut him off.

"Trip," she began with tears in her eyes. "You don't get it. He had to finish this off himself. I'm going to lose him to her again. Don't you see!?! Bruce is going to kill him!!" Jessica knew she was starting to get hysterical. Trip grabbed her shoulders. She stared right into his eyes. "I can't lose both of them," she said quietly.

"You're not going to," Chet said. He had walked up to them while Jessica was talking to Trip. He still looked a little green, but he pressed on. "We're going to stop him. This ends here, tonight. We get retribution for Sam. What happened to John and Sam is our fault, and we all know it. This is our burden to bear for the rest of our lives." He grabbed his phone and started dialing it. Jessica knew what he was trying to do but didn't even bother to warn him. She started back towards the car with the two of them following. Trip was thinking, and Chet pulled the phone away from his ear and looked at it while the voice said, "Hi, Worrywart." Jessica smiled in spite of herself. Trip snapped his fingers, and the other two turned toward him.

"This Thing of Ours," Trip said quietly. Chet looked at Trip and nodded.

"Yeah, Trip, it is," Chet replied. Trip looked irritated and shook his head.

"No, the bar, This Thing of Ours . . . wasn't that where John thought that Ricardo Antony found out that John was undercover?" Trip asked.

"Yeah," Chet replied, not understanding what Trip was saying.

"Don't you see? We found Ricardo's body just yesterday, but he had been dead for over a week, and it looked like he had been tortured," Trip explained. Chet still didn't understand.

"You think Bruce has been setting this up for a while then?" Jessica asked.

Trip turned towards her, nodding. "Exactly! John's probably walking into a trap." Jessica started running to the car with Trip and Chet following. She stopped, turned toward Chet and gave her orders.

"If you throw up in this car, I'll make you clean it for a month!! Do you understand me!?"

"Yes ma'am," Chet answered.

John Fowler
This Thing of Ours Bar – New York

Chapter 100

John shot back the drink and stared at Bruce.

"You look me right in the eyes, and tell me what happened!!" John screamed. He was beyond fury or anger. His body felt like it was burning. White, hot anger raced through every vein in his body. This was something he had never felt. John had no doubt in his mind if he got loose, he was going to kill Bruce. John wanted Bruce to die right in front of him. He had never understood some people's thirst for vengeance, until today. Bruce was going to die; John just didn't know how or when, yet. Bruce poured John another shot. Bruce nodded toward the drink. John glared at Bruce and drank the shot.

"Good boy," sneered Bruce. "This is how it's going to work. I'll tell you a piece of a little story and then pour you a drink. After you take each drink, I'll keep the story going. If you stop drinking, I stop telling you my story. Deal?" Bruce poured a drink and waited. John took the drink, his hand trembling. John shot it back. He was already beginning to physically sway. It had been almost four years since he drank alcohol, and Bruce knew John's tolerance level wasn't what it once was. The sick grin covered Bruce's face. John wanted to knock it off but knew he had to hear the whole story.

"John, I'm sorry. I mean, I hate your guts and wish a Mack truck would run over you, but what happened had absolutely nothing to do with you, and for that, I'm truly sorry." Bruce threw his head back and laughed. John felt his stomach churning. He thought he would throw up.

"She was carrying my child, you sick monster!" John spat.

Bruce bobbed his head from side to side with a remorseful look on his face.

"Yeah," Bruce said like a kid who had gotten his hand caught in a candy jar. "About that, I heard. Look, I'm really sorry. But think of it this way, John. I probably did you a favor. I mean, you're an alcoholic. Would you want to raise a child in that kind of home?" John was making a low guttural noise like a dog ready to pounce. Bruce held his hands up as if to say stop. "Ok, ok, so say you got help. We both know you loved the FBI too much to be a proper father. I mean, we both know you're the prima donna that has to be in the spotlight."

Bruce was eyeing John with pure pleasure.

"All of those pictures you took with Daddy dearest," said Bruce. "All of those times you rubbed my nose in it." Bruce was rubbing his hands together gleefully. "I took your life away, and I almost finished off your career if it hadn't been for that blasted Archibald Staples and his stupid daughter. Archibald had to pull you out of retirement to protect his little girl. You know what the kicker of it is, John? If Veronica, or Lisa, or whatever she's going by this week, had died when that maniac invaded the White House, then she never would have been in a position to blurt out Daddy's secrets. If that hadn't happened, the Senator doesn't get kidnapped. I wouldn't have had to kill Thelma or Dr. Freeman and let you bumbling idiots get close to figuring this all out. If that idiot Archibald had let David shoot her, we would have never gotten here!"

Bruce slammed his hand on the bar. The anger welled up in his face. He stared at John, and then, he smiled evilly. Bruce poured John another drink. John drank the shot down. Bruce didn't think John was going to last much longer. That brought the sick grin back to his face.

"Let me go on record; it was me who let David George out. I can't wait until he kills that snot daughter of Archibald's." Bruce walked behind the bar slowly, measuring how well John was able to track him with his eyes. "I have to admit that while I am sorry for what I have done to you, I have enjoyed seeing you build yourself back up, only to take everything away from you again."

Bruce poured another drink and motioned for John to drink. John reached for the drink, spilling a little of it. He steadied himself and drank down the shot. Bruce leaned in very close. He barely spoke above a whisper.

"John . . . I broke her pretty little neck."

Chet, Trip, and Jessica
Outside of This Thing of Ours Bar

Chapter 101

Jessica came to a stop just across the street from This Thing of Ours Bar. She jumped out of the car, gun drawn. Trip leaped out of the passenger seat, sprinted to her side, and pushed her gun down. She whipped around to look at Trip, staring daggers at him.

"Jessica," Trip pleaded. "You need to calm down. We can't barge in there without knowing the situation."

"The situation is I am going to shoot Bruce! That's the situation! I could care less about protocols and the FBI right now! That's the situation!" Jessica spat. "That fool is about to get himself killed. He's about to get himself killed over his dead wife. Doesn't he understand? She's gone! I'm here! Me! I loved Sam, too! Doesn't he get that?"

Chet watched silently, watching his partner, teammate, but more importantly, friend, become hysterical. He knew years ago when the three of them were first introduced to each other that there were sparks between Jessica and John, but never did he imagine he would see this. Jessica and Sam were closer than some sisters, and they both loved the same man. Chet swore to himself if he got the chance, he was going to take out Bruce for what he had done to his friends. Trip's words broke his thoughts.

"Jessica," Trip began calmly. "You can't go in there like this."

"You try and stop me," Jessica said quietly but forcefully. She started toward the door. "Call in reinforcements, Trip. I'm going in." Chet and Trip looked at each other. Chet shrugged and headed after her. Trip called it in and followed behind. It wasn't until they reached the door that Jessica noticed that both men were with her. She smiled a tight smile at them and nodded.

"We go in quietly," Trip said. Jessica nodded. A gun shot went off, and shock registered on each of their faces. Jessica recovered first and kicked the door opened. The three poured into the bar, hoping that their friend wasn't dead.

Chapter 102

John lost control after Bruce's confession and decided to try to take him out. Bruce dodged back as John swung wildly at him. John fell off the stool. He laid half on the ground as one arm hung in the air, still cuffed to the bar. John rested for a minute and pulled himself up where Bruce had sat the bottle in front of him. John picked it up and tried to measure the distance between them. Bruce had stepped well out of range of John swinging the bottle at him. Bruce made a sign for John to drink it down. John grabbed the bottle and began to chug. As he finished it all, Bruce drew a gun on John. Bruce reached in his pocket and grabbed a set of keys and slid them down the bar. John was shaking. It took some time for him to get the key in the lock. As he was doing this, Bruce began to speak.

"Daddy thought he was going to run for President. How?? How could he!?!? How could he with an illegitimate daughter? Mr. Conservative!! Other candidates, it would have never hurt them, but not dear old Daddy. He would have been ripped to pieces. I can hear it now. The most upstanding family man to run for office in 50 years has an illegitimate child," Bruce spat. "I did him a favor. I killed my half-sister, and then, I stole that bottle," pointing at the bottle John had just finished drinking from. "I knew I might have good use for it one day. I thought the explosion was a nice touch to end things with a pretty little bow, given how the mob thing had gone down." Bruce stood there a second, looking proud of himself.

"You never suspected me. You never thought another member of the FBI could ever be involved in something like this," Bruce scoffed. "If only you had cooperated and drank yourself to death, John. You have to make things so hard."

"She wasn't your sister," John slurred. Bruce looked at John in shock.

"Are you sure?" Bruce asked. John nodded the best he could. Bruce threw his head back and laughed. He roared with laughter. "So I killed her for nothing!?!? Whoopsie! My bad, bro!" Bruce continued to laugh hysterically. He reached under the bar and pulled out John's gun. He slid it down the bar, with his gun still trained on John.

"Now, here's what you're going to do. You're going to slowly pick up the gun with two fingers and lower it to your side. When I tell you, we're going to draw. I know, I know, it's so Old West. We don't have holsters, but it will still be fun. See, I can tell everyone you went on a drunken spell, admitted that you killed Sam, and then tried to kill me to keep me quiet." John picked up the gun like he was told as Bruce was speaking and slowly lowered it to his side. He gripped the gun correctly. Bruce lowered his gun to his side. It was all John could do not to smile as he spoke.

"Bruce, I only have one question," John said, slurring his words.

"What's that?" Bruce asked.

"Who says I'm drunk?" John asked in a strong, sober voice as he raised his gun. Bruce's face was painted with shock. Bruce froze, and John fired one shot into Bruce's right shoulder. Bruce spun and hit the ground. The doors behind John suddenly burst open. John turned, and there was Jessica, Trip, and Chet with their guns drawn. They lowered them as they saw John had the situation in hand.

John walked towards Jessica, Trip and Chet smiling. John pulled a digital recorder out of his pocket and flipped it to Trip. Trip looked at it strangely.

240

"I started it the moment I walked in this bar," John said. "I figured it was a trap, and I figured that if Bruce was guilty, he would want to gloat over me before he tried to finish me off. My biggest worry was that I didn't turn it on. I never expected you three to come help me." John looked down at the ground and then back at them. "Thank you," he said softly. John looked at Jessica and smiled at her. "I'm sorry. I had to do this myself." Jessica closed her eyes and shook her head. She opened them and got ready to chew on John. He held up his hand to cut her off.

"Sam won in the end," John said. The three of them looked confused.

"The drink she made that was in the bottle was non-alcoholic," John said as he pointed to the bottle on the bar and continued. "The idiot never checked to make sure it was real alcohol." John was shaking from the adrenaline wearing off. He took a deep breath and explained. "We were going to drink that bottle to celebrate the Mafia bust. She was going to tell me we were going to have a child. Don't you see? She couldn't drink because she was pregnant, and she never would have encouraged me to drink alcohol. Jess, she had her own program she had made for me, and I think it would have worked." John had tears in his eyes; so did Jessica. She was nodding her head in agreement with him. That was exactly the kind of thing Sam would have done. "Jess, I choose you. She's gone, this is finished, and I choose you. I don't know what else to do to convince you." John opened his arms to hug Jessica.

Jessica couldn't believe it. They had finally caught the murderer of Sam, and John had survived. She knew she should be mad, but she was so happy to see that she was wrong and John had survived. She opened her arms but flinched when she heard a gun-shot and something whiz by her. John had a strange look on his face. He looked down, and a red spot was spreading across his chest. John looked confused. He dropped to his knees, and Jessica saw Bruce behind him holding a gun. He smiled at her evilly, aiming his gun at Jessica. Jessica was frozen in place. Suddenly, Bruce's body shook with convulsions as three shots rang out and struck him. Chet, who had fired the shots into Bruce, crossed the room quickly, and kicked the gun away from him. Trip, who had been too stunned to shoot at Bruce, quickly holstered his gun, and called for an ambulance. Jessica dropped to the floor in front of John. John fell into her. As she held him, John looked into her eyes.

"Jess, I love you . . ." John shut his eyes.

"John? John!! JOHN!!!!!!!"

Sirens pierced the air as she heard Trip on the phone talking to someone.

"JOHN!!!!!!!"

The End . . .?

(No, it isn't.)

(The story continues in:
Journey's End
A Jessica Hammerstein Novel
~~A John Fowler Novel~~)

Author's Note

A little over a year ago, I put fingers to keyboard and began to write what I thought was going to be a short little story about an evil woman killing someone else for who she was. That story was terrible. It's just the plain, simple truth. But what came out of that story was the tale of John Fowler, a simple tale of redemption. I'm going to let you in on a little secret. John was supposed to die at the end of the book, taking a bullet for the first lady. A few friends began to read the book before I ever got to the end, and they encouraged me to make this into something more. For that, I can never thank them enough. So when I got to the end of book one, I knew what I had to do. I began to write what ended up being the end of this book The last part of this book that is about John and Bruce was 90% written at the same time book 1 was finished.

The question I kept getting when people found out about how this book was ending was why? Why would you kill John? Some think John isn't dead. Here's the truth. When I started writing book 4, I wrote the first 25 chapters twice. One in which John lives, and one in which John dies. Why would I do that? Let me answer that question with a question. What makes a hero? Someone who would give the ultimate sacrifice.

For all of you who want to find me and beat me right now, I simply ask you to read book 4 first. John's story will live on through him, or his team. The great J. M. DeMathis, an awesome comic book writer, once said something along the lines of, "What makes a great story? You put the hero through as many situations that seem impossible as you can. When it's over, the hero is much stronger."

I may not write a great literary work, but I have always strived to tell the best story in the world. That is my simple goal. Over 300 purchases and over 2,500 downloads of The Road to Justice worldwide makes me think some of you like what you're reading. My promise to you is that I will continue this series as long as I can think up stories that benefit the characters. I currently have this series mapped out into three, three-part acts. (You may blame George Lucas for that.) All I can tell you, if you think the way I ended 3 was bad, wait until you see 6.

Thank you all for the support, love, emails, texts, Facebook comments, and most of all buying the books. I know I'll never be a bestseller, but I appreciate each and every one of you taking the time to read my work! Thank you all, and God bless each of you.

David Carner